A

CANDLELIGHT REGENCY SPECIAL

CANDLELIGHT REGENCIES

216 A Gift of Violets, JANETTE RADCLIFFE
221 The Raven Sisters, DOROTHY MACK
225 The Substitute Bride, DOROTHY MACK
227 A Heart Too Proud, LAURA LONDON
232 The Captive Bride, LUCY PHILLIPS STEWART
239 The Dancing Doll, JANET LOUISE ROBERTS
240 My Lady Mischief, JANET LOUISE ROBERTS
245 La Casa Dorada, JANET LOUISE ROBERTS
246 The Golden Thistle, JANET LOUISE ROBERTS
247 The First Waltz, JANET LOUISE ROBERTS
248 The Cardross Luck, JANET LOUISE ROBERTS
250 The Lady Rothschild, SAMANTHA LESTER
251 Bride of Chance, LUCY PHILLIPS STEWART
253 The Impossible Ward, DOROTHY MACK
255 The Bad Baron's Daughter, LAURA LONDON
257 The Chevalier's Lady, BETTY HALE HYATT
263 Moonlight Mist, LAURA LONDON
501 The Scandalous Season, NINA PYKARE
505 The Bartered Bride, ANNE HILLARY
512 Bride of Torquay, LUCY PHILLIPS STEWART
515 Manner of a Lady, CILLA WHITMORE
521 Love's Captive, SAMANTHA LESTER
527 Kitty, JENNIE TREMAINE
530 Bride of a Stranger, LUCY PHILLIPS STEWART
537 His Lordship's Landlady, CILLA WHITMORE
542 Daisy, JENNIE TREMAINE
543 The Sleeping Heiress, PHYLLIS PIANKA
548 Love in Disguise, NINA PYKARE
549 The Runaway Heiress, LILLIAN CHEATHAM
554 A Man of Her Choosing, NINA PYKARE
555 Passing Fancy, MARY LINN ROBY

Thomasina

JOAN VINCENT

A Candlelight Regency Special

Published by
Dell Publishing Co., Inc.
1 Dag Hammarskjold Plaza
New York, New York 10017

ISBN: 0-440-18844-X

Printed in the United States of America

First printing—May 1980

To Vera, THE UNKNOWING INSTIGATOR
To Vince, THE SURPRISING SUPPORTER
To Carolyn, THE UNDAUNTED CONFIDANTE
To Barb, THE PROFESSORIAL PROOFREADER

CHAPTER 1

Laughter trailed in bubbling echoes after the pair of schoolroom truants. Bright midafternoon sunshine pierced the trees they were running through, dappling the ground and infecting their gaiety.

The young boy freed his hand from the grasp of his companion and burst forward in triumph. Picking up her skirts, the young woman gave chase. It took a furlong before she came within reach of him; panting had replaced the laughter. A desperate lunge put her hands on the boy's shoulders just at the moment he decided to end the race by dropping to the ground. She frantically attempted to vault over him but succeeded only in tumbling down, her legs foiled by her petticoats.

"Parker, that was decidedly unfair," the young woman complained, striving to untangle herself from the nuisance petticoats while the cause for her tumble lay doubled over with glee.

"Tommi," he gasped through his laughter, "that was splendid!"

A rueful smile appeared as Thomasina realized this was one of the few times the boy had been genuinely pleased about anything. She plucked at the small twigs and blades of grass that were tangled in her soft, fair-hued copper curls.

Parker rolled onto his stomach and propped his chin in his hands. Mischievous delight twinkled in his wide blue eyes—a look Thomasina had seen all too often since her arrival at her uncle's home ten months past.

"Wait until mama sees you, Tommi," Parker intoned seriously. "You will be required to dine in the schoolroom for a fortnight."

Thomasina halted picking the leafy debris

off her skirt and watched the boy's features closely. *Could it be,* she wondered, *that he desires company—my company?* That he would do anything in seeking his parents' attention was beyond doubt; his behaviour ranged from utterly despicable to awkwardly loveable, and almost all of it kept her in the bad graces of her aunt. Standing, she said, "You must play here for a short time, Parker. The fresh air will be very beneficial, and I must try and repair my toilet."

"What is there for me to do?" he snapped, turning sullen at not having raised her ire.

"Run, jump. See how many different kinds of blades of grass or leaves you can find. We could look up what they are when we return to the schoolroom," she added in despairing optimism.

To her surprise, Parker obediently bounded away.

She sighed and turned her eyes from him to her dress. It was fortunate, she thought, that she had chosen one of her own older day frocks instead of one of those that her cousin, Dianna, had haughtily ordered the abigail to bring to her. Thomasina shook her skirt with more vigour than necessary as she thought of Dianna.

"I will not allow her to make me miserable," she said softly to herself. "I will not. No matter how much she talks of her London season."

Having brushed the last of the greenery from her skirt and given a grimace to the irremovable grass stains, Thomasina looked about. Parker was still playing within her sight; it would be safe to rest. Seating herself next to a large tree, she leaned back against it. The fresh stem of grass she plucked was tasty. Swirling it over her tongue, she closed her eyes.

Visions from the past leapt out of the secreted chambers of her mind, confronting her as they were wont to do since her mother's death, thirteen months before.

The tall, slim figure of her father appeared first—he was laughing as he entered their cottage and grabbed hold of her mother, singing and twirling her about the small parlour. Her mother's face was lit with that cautious joy that always greeted her father's happier homecomings. Thomasina had learned early in her life that his euphoria seldom lasted beyond a week, and then he would be gone again.

The panorama of her mind shifted to the familiar scene of her mother seated in the old ebony rocker before the open fire of the kitchen, leaning towards it, trying to catch the light as she stitched.

Thomasina's eyes flashed open, bidding the scene away. *At what age,* she asked herself, *did I realize it was mother's needlework and the kindness of neighbors that kept food in our larder? When did I know father for the weak, irresolute man he was?* Shaking her head sadly, she closed her eyes once more.

Immediately the next scene presented itself—all too vividly real. There she was, returning to the small cottage, smiling because she knew her mother would be pleased; Lady Glaxton had liked the work and had given two shillings extra for it. The door opened and she called out, but her mother did not answer.

In the tiny cottage it did not take her long to find her mother, rooted to a chair in the parlour.

"Mother," Thomasina said, sinking on her knees before the chair. "Mother, are you ill?"

A lone tear stood on one of her mother's cheeks. "I am sorry, Thomasina," she said very softly.

"Come, mother. Let me help you to bed," Thomasina urged.

"Your father has died—he . . . he killed himself after losing the little we had left to Lord Longeton. Everything is the Marquess's now. I am sorry, child—you shall have no home," came faintly from the alabaster figure of a woman.

Staring in frightening comprehension, Thomasina saw her mother's face become set and her hand slide from the chair's arm to dangle in the air.

As she jumped up, Thomasina shook the painful reality of the past from her. Angrily, she sermonized herself for thinking back. Her mother's oft-repeated lesson echoed in her ears: "The futilest of futile actions is looking back and wanting what is lost forever." Channeling her anger into a demi-hatred of Lord Longeton, she told herself how grateful she must be that her mother's brother was willing to take her in charge. *At least,* she thought with a bitter smile, *I will not have to concern myself with men or marriage.* Dowerless, no one would give her a second look and this, she reasoned, was a true blessing. She did not want to repeat her mother's fate, and even a more materially-endowed marriage, such as that of her aunt and uncle, was less than pleasant. At one and twenty, Thomasina had willingly resigned herself to spinsterhood.

A faint "Tommi" came to her ear, breaking her reverie.

Parker, she thought. What has he gotten into now? she asked herself as she hastened toward his panicked calling. Thomasina frowned as she saw the dark brown of the beaten path visitors sometimes used on their way to and from Buckley House contrasted against the verdant grass. They had come much too far. Surveying the large trees that stood along either side of the path, thickly grown over with vines, she sought sight of Parker.

"I am up here, Tommi," the boy called.

"Where?" she called back in return.

"Look up. Up here!"

"Parker Buckley! What are you doing in that tree?" scolded Thomasina as her eyes finally located the boy midway up in the largest tree near her.

"I am frightened, Tommi. I cannot come down," he whined.

"Of course you can come down," she said firmly. "Follow the course you took in going up the tree."

"I am afraid. I will fall, I know it! You must come and help me, Tommi. Please!"

"I am not dressed for climbing trees," Thomasina scoffed. "Stop this nonsense and come down."

"If you will not come and help me down, you must fetch father and some of the servants to do so. I know I shall fall and die if I let go."

Thomasina lowered her head to ease her aching neck and considered the situation. Parker sounded miserable enough; perhaps this was not another of his pranks, she thought. Her eyes took in the tree. It was a perfect specimen for climbing, with its viny cover and ladderway of limb crotches. Possibly . . .

Making one last attempt to avoid having to fetch him, she said, "Parker, you know you can come down by yourself. You can reach from one vine to another as you make your way down. Please try."

"I shall fall and die! You just want to be rid of me," the boy wailed agitatedly.

Thomasina looked up and down the path as she called to Parker to calm himself. It would not do to have someone come along and find them treed—after all, they were supposed to be in the schoolroom.

"All right, Parker. I will come—stay still now." Coming as near to a curse as she knew how, Thomasina gathered her overskirt and the top two petticoats into a bunch. These she secured about her waist with her long sash belt. "Perfectly scandalous," she piped, mimicking Aunt Augusta as she surveyed the result. With a last note of Parker's position, she slipped her shoes from her feet and began the climb.

"Hurry, Tommi, hurry!" Parker called anxiously.

"Do not fear, Parker, I am almost there," Thomasina answered as she paused briefly. In a few seconds she was on the same branch as the boy but, still distrustful of the reality of his plight, stayed next to the main trunk of the tree. "Come to me, Parker," she ordered, reaching out her hand.

"I cannot," he wailed, summoning two huge tears to the fore. "If I take even one step without you to hold on to, I shall die!"

"Nonsense," Thomasina snapped. She saw the boy's head cock, then heard the dull thump of a casually loping steed. They must not be seen here. Pushing aside all doubts and caution, she edged towards the boy, who stood just beyond mid-limb.

"Grab that vine above you, Tommi," Parker urged. "You will be safe from falling then."

Looking up she saw the tail of a vine dangling just within her reach and caught it with one hand.

"No—take hold of it with both hands, tightly," Parker urged, suddenly edging towards her as the hoofbeats neared. "I will take hold of your waist."

Not wishing to delay matters, Thomasina gritted her teeth and, with the vine firmly in the grip of both hands, she edged to the boy's side.

Parker gripped her waist but would not move as she began to step back to the tree's main trunk. Instead he braced himself in the opposite direction and screamed "Help!" at the top of his lungs.

Panic set in as Thomasina tried desperately to drag him with her, murderous thoughts streaming through her mind at his treachery.

He tugged at her, screeching all the while. Fear of discovery left Thomasina's mind as the scuffle changed from attempting to pry the boy loose to keeping her footing. As she wavered wildly she vaguely heard Parker yell, "Watch out below, sir!" Then her mind momentarily blanked as she slipped and fell from the limb. The vine she clutched for security fell with her as she dropped in a wide arc across the path. It jerked her to an abrupt halt ten feet above the ground right before the galloping mount that reared at her sudden appearance. The gentleman atop the steed controlled his mount easily and then proceeded to survey the shapely, hosed ankles and calves of the dangling, and thunderously angry, Thomasina. He noted the odd adjustment of her skirt and petticoats and the lack of shoes. Thinking it had been a young boy who called for help, he scanned the upper branches of the tree but saw no one.

Twirling slowly and helplessly about, Thomasina's anger grew as she caught glimpses of the large, scowling man who merely sat watching her.

"The least you could do is help me down," she clipped through gritted teeth, as awareness of her appearance increased her discomfiture.

"And would you be suitably grateful, wench?" he asked unpleasantly. "The effort involved in your scheme does denote some recompense."

Thomasina's face flamed red as she sputtered indignantly.

This reaction brought a slight curve of the lip, which one familiar with the individual would have termed a smile. Directing his mount forward to Thomasina's side, he stood in the stirrups to his full height, reached up, and grasped her firmly about the waist. "You are secure now—release your grip on the vine."

Thomasina looked down into the dark, angular face. His emerald-green eyes bore through her.

"I said, let go of the vine," his voice commanded.

Involuntarily, Thomasina jerked her eyes from his to her hands. She let go of the vine as if it were a firebrand.

Relaxing into the saddle, the gentleman carried her down in his steely grip. "Now you must pay the price for my assistance—or get the reward for your effort—whichever thought agrees with your own."

Thomasina's eyes searched his face for a hint of his mad reasoning and saw his intent too late to prevent his lips from capturing her own.

In her surprise, seconds sped by before she erupted into a twisting, kicking bundle. The mount, startled by her sudden movements, reared, and Thomasina found herself released and dropped unceremoniously to the ground as the steed was once more brought under control.

Struggling upright, she saw the man's eyes upon her own, which were brown pools of flashing anger. They held her in their grip until he doffed his hat and said sarcastically, "May the next man you meet not have to pluck you from the tree like a 'green' apple. Good day." And he was gone.

"Who was that, Tommi?" called Parker as he scampered down the tree. "Who was it? Why did you permit him to kiss you?"

Thomasina rose and forced herself to untie her sash calmly, brushing her skirts down and smoothing her hair before she looked at the boy.

Parker edged closer and in a contrite tone asked, "You are unhurt, Tommi? I did not mean you any harm."

"We are going directly to your father when we get back to Buckley House," she answered, "and you are going to explain your reprehensible behaviour in this whole affair."

"But he will be angry, terribly angry."

"It does not matter."

"Are you not afraid of what he will do to you? He will send you away. Mama will make him when she learns of it," quaked a striken Parker.

"He can do as he pleases. What loss is it to you if I must go?"

"No, Tommi, you must stay! Please, let us say nothing. You know both mama and papa are being dreadfully out of sorts these days.

"I wish that old man would come and marry Dianna, and then she would go away and everything would be fine." He pouted. "Please, Tommi. I will not tell anyone, ever. Please?"

Thomasina glared at the boy coldly. Fear of his parents had caused him to blanch; at the worst, she had never had cause to fear her own. Her compulsion to tell of the happening weakened. It would go badly for him as well as for her if the incident became known. She might not be able to secure a position as governess, as was her hope, when Parker was sent to school in the fall.

The boy read the change in her and hugged her tightly. "Thank you, Tommi. I shall be good for you, you shall see." He turned his brightened face upwards to her. "Let us hurry back. I would like to see who father's caller is." Contriteness appeared once more as he saw Thomasina's reaction to this. "But not if you say I shouldn't." Turning, he started walking sedately in the direction of Buckley House.

Thomasina followed slowly. She had no desire to learn who the impudent caller was. *If fate be kind,* she thought. *I will never set eyes on that particular "gentleman" again.*

CHAPTER 2

"How good to see you, Lord Longeton," Baron Buckley greeted the tall, angular man who had just been ushered into his study. The Baron's smile faltered as it encountered the meditative broodiness of the other as he drew near.

"You received my letter," Longeton stated.

"Yes, my lord, although," the Baron cleared his throat, "although the meaning was not . . . well, not explicit."

"There should have been no misunderstanding my intent," Longeton declared, his eyes piercing the Baron, causing him to squirm inwardly.

"O-o-of c-course," stuttered the Baron, "it is not that I misunderstood. It is. . . ." He looked about abstractedly. "It is a bit early," he said, hoping for a more favourable response, "but could I offer you some refreshment? You must be tired and thirsty after your journey. Did you come by coach?" he asked as he poured two glasss of sherry.

"I rode," Longeton answered tonelessly as he accepted the glass.

The Baron stepped to the side of the room and pulled the bell cord. "It is so inconsiderate of me. I will have our man, Gill, show you to your rooms. After you have been introduced to Dianna this evening, we can speak more of the matter. We do dine rather early—country hours, you know." The words tumbled from the Baron's lips.

"Oh, Gill," he instructed as the butler entered, "escort Lord Longeton to his rooms. See to any and all of his needs.

"Will you have a coach arriving soon?" he asked Longeton, who nodded in reply.

"See to everything, Gill. Till we sup then, my lord."

Longeton paused momentarily as the babble ceased, considering bolting before the affair had progressed too far for a graceful exit. The whole purpose of his visit appeared ludicrous now that he had arrived. This action was stayed by the sudden flash of a vision of a pair of wickedly angry brown eyes and a tousled mop of copperish curls. He nodded curtly and followed Gill from the study.

As the echo of his lithe steps faded, the Baron returned to the sherry decanter and refilled his glass. Taking his seat behind his desk, he removed a kerchief and mopped his brow. Longeton was as disconcerting in Buckley House as he found him to be on the few occasions they came together while in London, the Baron thought. *The man is capable of looking through one or not seeing one as he wishes. How will I ever endure such a son-in-law? But then. . . .*

His thoughts were interrupted by the swish of petticoats. He quaffed his sherry, rose, and returned the glass to the decanter's side before his wife entered the room.

Lady Augusta Buckley came into the study under full sail. "Why was I not called?" she shrilled at her husband. "Brown told me Lord Longeton has arrived, and you did not even think to let me speak with him. You know this is of the utmost importance to us and, of course, to Dianna—what kind of impression did you make upon him?"

"Calm yourself, Augusta," the Baron interceded. "He wished to freshen up before meeting you and Dianna. We must remain calm and keep our wits about us."

"Yes, yes, as if you retained any of yours." She waved a bony hand at him. "You must be very careful to do nothing that will alter his lordship's intent in this affair." She wagged her head. "To think I despaired of her first season," the high-pitched voice continued. "I cannot recall a single instance when Longeton gave Dianna more than a passing glance. Why, 'pon my soul, he never bothered with any of the green girls."

"That does not matter now," the Baron interposed. "Think what having him for a son-in-law will do for us. It ensures Parker will travel in elite circles when he comes of age."

The Baroness agreed, "Yes, he will be quite a feather in our caps.

"If only we knew the reason he has chosen

Dianna," she minced. "He has not been out of mourning for more than a week—why would he be so abrupt in this? He must be infatuated with her."

"This is not a settled fact yet, my dear. Keep that daughter of yours in hand. He will not want a wife who will prove forward."

"There will be no problem with her. I have gone over her deportment lessons, and she is quite as excited about this opportunity as we are. Think—the Marchioness of Thornhill. No one will be able to snub me again if we achieve this match."

"Now, my dear—" began the Baron, hoping to forestall one of his wife's tirades on that subject.

"And it may be just the answer for Thomasina," interrupted Lady Augusta.

"You are quite correct. How brilliant for you to hit upon it. Dianna can sponser Thomasina for her season," complimented the Baron, relieved that her thoughts had been diverted.

"What?! I had no such thought in mind. The girl does not desire a season; it is unthinkable at her age. Why, she wishes me to find her a post as governess when Parker goes to school.

"No, she can be a companion for Dianna, and in only a short time there should be use for her as a nanny," Lady Augusta ended concisely.

Baron Buckley frowned but did not object. Over twenty years of marriage had taught him the futility of that.

"Now I must see to the selection of Dianna's gown for this evening and, of course, have Thomasina instructed that she and Parker will sup in the schoolroom. I believe the wisest course is to keep Parker from his lordship until the matter is settled; the boy is so unpredictable."

"Yes, my dear, whatever you think best," Buckley replied, paging once more through an open book before him.

"Must you dawdle all your time away on books?" Lady Augusta rebuked him before sailing from the room.

The Baron closed the book with a sigh as his wife's back disappeared from view. It was not oft that his thoughts turned to his family, but now they did so. He felt pride that he had achieved the possibility of such a grand match for his daughter; then his pride winced as he thought of his niece, Thomasina.

When word of her plight—father and mother gone and the cottage she called home a victim of the gaming tables—had reached him, his wife had respounded with unusual compassion. She had urged him to write and invite Thomasina to make her home with them, saying what a good companion the older girl would be for Dianna. Her intent, however, became clear as soon as the girl arrived. Thomasina was given the governess's chamber in the schoolroom and assigned the care of Parker, whom six previous governesses had not been able to endure. Lady Augusta and Dianna treated her as little better than a servant, and excuses were soon found for her not to accompany them on social calls or to travel to London for the season.

All these injustices goaded him and he decided that once Dianna's betrothal was announced to his lordship, he would ask Longeton's help in making a match for Thomasina; he would make up as best he could for all she had endured under his roof.

With his conscience placated for the moment, he dismissed the matter.

On the third floor of Buckley House, Parker and Thomasina were working on the day's lessons. Both were so relieved to have succeeded in making their way back to the schoolroom unobserved that they were plying the books with thankful concentration.

"Beggin' your pardon, miss," Lisa interrupted.

Thomasina's eyes swung up, encountering the tray-filled arms of the young serving maid. She cleared a space among the books and papers for her; Lisa had been one of the few in the household who had shown any amount of friendliness to her.

As she sat the tea and biscuits from the tray, Lisa babbled excitedly. "His lordship's come—the one they've been expectin'. The one they say is to marry with Miss Dianna. Oh, he's tall, but his looks are lost in that sombre grimace he carries with him. Mr. Gill took him to that grand blue suite, and he's not showed himself since."

Parker kept his head glued to his papers, and Thomasina tried to temper a frown.

"Now ain't you a fine pair!" Lisa teased lightly. "The whole household has been in an uproar, what with all the scrubbin' and shinin' and waxin' we've been doin' for what seems like weeks on end. Now neither of you can even ask who his lordship is."

"Did he come by way of the wood's path?" burst from Parker.

"Aye. I know because Mr. Gill was sayin' to Mrs. Brown how odd it was for his lordship to come alone and in the saddle. His coach is not to arrive until later this evenin'."

"Who is he?" the boy asked, despite Thomasina's glare.

"Ah, one grander than I'd have ever thought would take to the likes of Miss Dianna—" Lisa clasped her hand to her mouth "—beggin' your pardon, miss."

"What is his name?" insisted Parker.

"Well," said Lisa importantly, "he is a true blue blood—a marquess."

Thomasina felt her stomach fall. There was only one marquess she had ever heard any talk of, the one who had taken her home. But reason said it could not be the same man.

"The Marquess of Thornhill, Lord Longeton, himself," Lisa concluded. "To think

Miss Dianna will be a marchioness," she sighed.

"Longeton," was all Thomasina said.

Lisa looked at her, thinking her behaviour odd, for usually Thomasina was the merriest one in the house. "I'll be back for the tray as usual, miss." She bobbed a curtsy. "Oh, I was to tell you—you and Master Parker will be dining in the schoolroom this eve."

A long sigh of relief came from Thomasina, while a look of disappointment marked Parker's face as the door closed behind the maid.

I will at least be spared meeting the man, thought Thomasina, *but for how long?* That it was he, the one who had caused all she loved best to be lost, was nearly incomprehensible. How could she meet him civilly?

Parker misread her perturbation. "I meant it when I promised I would not tell anyone what happened, Tommi. No one will ever learn it from me."

The boy's words brought the demanding movement of Longeton's lips to Thomasina's mind, and she raised a hand to her own. Lowering it quickly, she forced a weak smile. "I do not doubt it, Parker. Let us have our tea and then you can finish the last of your lesson." The steady hand that poured the tea belied the agitation swirling through her being.

CHAPTER 3

Conversation at the Buckley supper table was dull, strained, and sporadic. Lord Longeton was not proving a talkative guest, and Lady Augusta was about to despair of the situation.

Dianna, overawed by his lordship's title and brooding demeanour, had done little but stare at the space of table before her and devour whatever was placed upon it ever since they had seated themselves.

Silence reigned as the last course was served; even Lady Augusta for once was wordless. Longeton watched as Dianna attacked the serving before her and wondered how he could ever have let himself be convinced that this was the girl for whose hand he should apply. She had not uttered more than four syllables all evening and those four were interspersed with girlish giggles. His lordship's mind quaked at the thought of a lifetime shackled to a nonspeaking, steadily eating wife. There was nothing for him to do but make his apologies and leave in the morning before the subject of his letter could be broached.

"I apologize for the lack of company this evening, Lord Longeton," Lady Augusta began in her strident nasal tones. "The table will be much improved tomorrow with the addition of several of our neighbors. There are among their number members of Parliament and, of course, Lord Sherrad. His land borders ours on the west, you know. I am certain all would welcome the opportunity to visit with someone recently come from London." Concluding, she threw a prodding glance at her husband.

"I say, Longeton, do you hunt?" the Baron rushed out. "I dare say we could have the servants raise something, even at this time of year. Sherrad and his sons have good hunters and, I dare say, mine are capital."

Searching his mind for a properly phrased refusal, Longeton began to feign a sudden relish for the dish before him.

The silence, once more ensconced in the room, was broken by a shrill, boyish scream for help.

The call struck a cord of recognition in Lord Longeton. He glanced at the other three seated at the table with him; all were intent upon their plates.

"Perhaps we should see what the trouble is," he noted, feeling an excitement foreign to him.

"It is nothing, I am sure, your lordship. Certainly nothing you should trouble yourself with," Lady Augusta managed smoothly, despite the dull red tinge of her cheeks. "The servants will see to it."

"Help!" echoed clearly through the open doors at the end of the dining room once more.

The Baron felt a vicious kick to his shin. Question and pain covered his features until he saw his wife's face. Pushing back his chair he excused himself. "Will only take a moment," he muttered as he laboured around the table, favouring his offended leg, and made for the open doors.

"I will join you. Excuse me, Lady Buckley, Miss Dianna," Longeton said, laying his napkin down and rising in one smooth motion.

He and the Baron were through the doors before Lady Augusta recovered herself enough to object.

"Thomasina has spoiled it all," whined Dianna.

"Shut up," snapped her mother. "You have done little better, sitting there like a . . . like a bird being stuffed."

Dianna winced and tears came to the fore.

"Now is no time for that foolishness," commanded her mother sternly. "You know how crying affects your appearance. Of course, Thomasina is at fault and she shall be called to attention for it. Straighten yourself, child, and think—think of what you can say to his lordship."

Dusk had not completely vanished as the Baron and Lord Longeton emerged onto the terrace from the dining room. A faint rose-coloured light was lying over the gardens before them.

Both men stood still listening intently. A scuffling sound behind and above them turned Longeton's head. He caught only a brief glimpse of a young boy being hauled through an open window, but the mop of copperish curls atop the one assisting the boy was unmistakable. A glimmer of a smile lit his features.

The Baron's eyes had followed Longeton's and had seen his son being pulled through the window. Hesitantly, he turned towards the Marquess and was encouraged by what he saw. Mistaking the reason for the smile, he chuckled weakly saying, "We all recall our boyhood days . . . have all misbehaved at one time or another. Parker is a bit more active than most boys his age. . . ." He halted as he saw the question rise in Longeton's eyes.

"Parker is my son and Thomasina does have trouble handling him at times," he explained. "Not that I hold her responsible, after all."

Looking back to the now empty window, Longeton asked, "Thomasina?"

"She is not to be blamed for Parker's misdeeds—my niece, you know. Lost her parents a little more than a year ago. Shortly before your brother passed away, God rest his soul, come to think of it." Longeton's suddenly darkening brow at the mention of his brother led the Baron to drop the subject. "Perhaps it would be best if we reenter and let the matter—" he tilted his head towards the window "—remain with us."

"You have beautifully arranged gardens," Longeton said obtusely. "How fortunate the call bid us forth—" he paused "—even though there was no one or nothing to be seen."

The Baron raised his brows appreciatively.

"You will have to show me the gardens tomorrow and of course, I will have to give one of your hunters a go," continued Longeton as he took the Baron's elbow and led the way back into the dining room.

"Lady Augusta, what excellent taste has been shown in your gardens. Dianna and yourself must take me on a tour of them tomorrow."

These words had the desired effect of making the two ladies forget the interruption and the meal was concluded to everyone's satisfaction.

"It is the same man," Parker whispered as he stood planted firmly against the wall of the schoolroom next to the window where Thomasina had thumped him moments before.

Words from below came faintly through the window; there were steps, then silence.

Thomasina slowly relaxed and Parker, daring to move forward, found his shoulder in a tight grasp.

"I only wanted to see if it was the same man, Tommi. You know mother will not allow us to meet him."

"For which we should be thankful! He is not the kind of man who would let me forget the incident along the path. He would relish my humiliation and your punishment," Thomasina declared vehemently.

"You are only angry because he kissed you," retorted Parker.

"No!"

The tone of Thomasina's voice and her unnatural harshness of expression silenced the boy. "Very well," he said slowly. "Do not be angry with me, Tommi. Please?"

Thomasina's shoulders sagged as if under a great weight. "I am not, Parker. Only fatigued. Go fetch your nanny and have her ready you for bed. I will tuck you in when you are ready."

"Yes, Tommi," answered Parker as he went to the door. Looking back at Thomasina he hesitated, but left without further words.

With her hand to her brow, Thomasina walked slowly to the open window through which she had so recently jerked Parker to safety. The thought of the danger he had been in, in trying to climb down the wall to peek through the dining room doors, was lost to her as she looked down on the empty terrace below.

A soft glow flickered a short distance from the open doors of the dining room, wavering as it attempted to pierce the darkness.

Looking down into the blackening backdrop, Thomasina's mind saw his angular visage once more—and recalled the deep emerald of his eyes. She lowered her hand slowly to her heart. It was her hatred of him that caused such a vivid recollection of his features and such a rapid beat of her heart, she assured herself, nothing more.

CHAPTER 4

Lord Longeton's valet, Gideon, watched his master with dimly concealed interest. Noting his lordship was taking unusual pains with his appearance this morn, Gideon could only presume that Lord Longeton had proven human at last.

Gideon's thoughts were not an indication of disrespect, for there was no man living for whom he had more respect, but he and his lordship's history together was long and he had the desire (common to all men) to see a man perceived as less than human to be proven more than human.

The valet's admiration for the as yet unseen Miss Buckley grew with each new cravat that he handed the Marquess. At last the desired effect was achieved and Lord Longeton departed his rooms.

Gill encountered Lord Longeton in the upper hall and directed him to the breakfast room. There the Marquess found Baron Buckley, generously heaping his plate from the abundant sources on the sideboard. Neither spoke until both had made their choices and seated themselves.

Encouraged by Longeton's friendly demeanour, the Baron began. "Slept well, I take it—looking very fit this morn," he gabbled on between mouthfuls.

Longeton nodded affirmation and asked, "Will we take breakfast alone, or will your family join us—your wife, perhaps?"

"I dare say I hope not," said the Baron, his fork frozen in the air midway to his mouth. "Augusta—Lady Buckley, is quite . . . er . . . quite a late riser," he finished as he chomped onto his forkful of meat. "And Dianna never. . . . Well, I mean, Thomasina will have been ordered. . . . Yes, we dine alone," he concluded firmly, hoping the subject done.

"Your niece," Longeton asked casually, "does she take all her meals in the schoolroom then?"

The opening of the door interrupted them and both men stood as a surprised Thomasina halted her entry in mid-step.

"Come in, child, we will not eat you—you can see there is plenty else," laughed the Baron.

"Your pardon, Uncle," stammered Thomasina. "I did not think his lordship would be about. . . ." She waved her hand as if to clear her momentary confusion and took a step backwards.

"I regret that my presence disconcerts you, Miss. . . ." Longeton looked to the Baron, realizing he had not been told Thomasina's family name.

"Oh, balderdash. Tommi, come in here this instant," blustered the Baron. "How am I to make a proper introduction with you having one foot in and one foot out? One would think you were ready to bolt from an ogre.

"You must not mind her, Longeton—not used to society, you know."

Thomasina's faint blush darkened at her uncle's words, but she saw no way to escape. Deciding that to deter was to worsen her fate, she raised her gaze proudly, albeit somewhat belligerently, at Lord Longeton and entered the room.

"That is better. Lord Longeton, may I present my niece, Miss Thomasina Thait. Tommi, this is Lord Brutus Longeton, the Marquess of Thornhill."

As Thomasina forced herself into the slightest of curtsies, she was startled by his lordship moving from his stance by the table to her side.

He means to tell Uncle, she thought wildly and was even more astounded when he reached out his hand before her expectantly. As if mesmerized, she placed her hand lightly in his to find it firmly captured as her mind ordered it withheld.

Longeton kissed it lightly and after a momentary pause released it. Picking up a plate, he said, "Please be seated, Miss Thait. It will give me pleasure to make your choices for you."

Baron Buckley motioned Thomasina towards him. She threw his lordship an angry frown, went to the Baron, and let him seat her.

"Relax, Tommi," her uncle whispered. "It is time you learned how one conducts oneself in society. His lordship is merely being civil."

Thomasina directed her eyes to her lap, realizing her uncle must have completely forgotten Longeton's disastrous association with her father and its resultant cause of her mother's death.

The Marquess's light, manish cologne penetrated her senses; she felt the brush of his arm against her shoulder as he served her plate with a slight flourish.

"I hope my choices will prove satisfactory," he said pleasantly.

"You could not have done better," the Baron's voice boomed into Thomasina's consciousness. "Exactly the selection she would have made."

Forcefully focusing her attention on the filled plate, she realized the truth of her uncle's words, but it only served to make her view the generous servings as an insult, and her anger increased.

"She does not have the look of one who is a

finicky eater," Longeton commented matter-of-factly.

"No, no," laughed the Baron. "And well she does not, with that rascally son of mine she must deal with." He paused. "What is wrong?" he asked Thomasina, seeing that she had not raised a fork to any of her food.

"I . . . I do not have much appetite this morn, Uncle," she choked out.

"Nonsense. More than likely suffering from embarrassment," the Baron told the Marquess. "Usually she eats as heartily as I, although—" he winked broadly "—it has suited her frame more appropriately than mine."

Thomasina felt her face burning. Keeping her eyes lowered, she managed to swallow a few bites.

"The Baron tells me that you are acting as governess to his son, Miss Thait. Do you find the task enjoyable as well as fulfilling?" Longeton asked as he cut his beef, seeking to ease the embarrassment the Baron's words were causing her.

Misunderstanding his intent, Thomasina flashed a look of utter outrage and hatred across the table at him.

Raising his eyes as he slowly chewed his

beef, Longeton choked as he encountered the intenseness of her disfavour.

Baron Buckley rose and thumped him soundly on the back as he coughed, and Thomasina took advantage of the instance to disappear from the room.

"I am quite recovered," Longeton insisted loudly as the Baron continued his pounding.

"Ah, good," said the Baron, returning to his chair. "You gave me quite a fright, you know. Dangerous business, choking on meat. Had a friend who died doing that. Dangerous business."

"I heartily agree," returned Longeton as he arched his aching back; for all the Baron's flab, his arms still held their strength.

"Well now, where could Tommi have gone to? And her plate practically untouched. Deuced odd, that. I suppose she was unsettled by your company—we usually breakfast alone, she and I. Fine girl she is. I was wondering if you could help to— Well, I dare say that's best left unsaid for now," the Baron clacked on at his usual pace.

"What were we speaking of? Ah, yes, the kidney—excellent work our cook makes of it—don't you agree? But then, everyone to his own 'snuff' as it were. Let us make done with this, and I will take you to the stables so you can make your choice of mounts for this afternoon, unless you prefer your own.

"I have sent a message to Lord Sherrad. He may not be able to ride—gout, you know—but his sons will come. Fine boys they are—only a few years younger than yourself, I believe. The oldest must be all of five or six and twenty. Yes, fine lads, I have known them since their births. . . ."

Thomasina did not stop running until she was in the refuge of her own room. Closing the door firmly behind her, she leaned against it heavily.

What am I to do? she thought wildly. *What game is he making of this?* With tightly clasped hands, she paced the small open center of her room. Slowly, calm reasserted itself as she reasoned through the dilemma.

Longeton was not surprised at her appearance, she thought, so somehow he had learned of her presence here. *He has not told Uncle, that is certain. What can he mean to do? Toy with me as a mouser does its prey?* Yes, that would be the kind of foul play to expect from his sort. Well, he would find that this mouse had her own claws.

Going to the miserly-looking glass provided solely so that the governess would have no excuse for being anything but neat, she viewed her reflection. Beyond her own features a vague image of his lordship appeared and she stuck out her tongue, driving it from her mind's eye. "Brutus," she said aloud, "mythical first king of Britain. 'Belial,' worthless and wicked, would suit you better, my Lord Longeton.

" 'She does not have the look of one who is a finicky eater,' " Thomasina mimicked exaggeratedly and made another face in honour of his lordship.

A tapping at her door caused her to start guiltily. "Yes?" she answered, momentarily fearful her uncle was summoning her return to the breakfast room.

"Lady Buckley says you're to come to her sitting room at once," an undermaid called through the door. "Her ladyship says for the nanny to look after Master Parker while you do."

"Tell her I am coming," Thomasina answered, opening the door. "I will just check on my charge."

"You'd best hurry, miss. Her ladyship is . . . well. . . ."

"Thank you, I will," Thomasina smiled at the girl.

She could easily see how her aunt could intimidate a girl so fresh from an estate cottage. "Do not fear—I will be there shortly."

The young undermaid showed a meek smile of appreciation as she bobbed a curtsy and turned to go.

Thomasina closed the door and crossed the room, entering the schoolroom by a second connecting door. Parker was seated at the schoolroom table just finishing his breakfast.

"Good morn, Tommi," he said, greeting her with a gruel-covered smile.

"Good morn to you, Parker," Thomasina returned, "and see it remains a good morn for all. Good morn, Nanny," she added to the old woman who had stood as she entered.

"Good morn, Miss Thomasina," the wizened woman answered with a bob.

"Lady Augusta seeks my presence this morn," Thomasina said in explanation. "Parker may play about the room until I return." She turned to him. "Behave yourself," she cautioned the boy.

"I shan't be long, Nanny."

"Don't you be lettin' her frighten you, miss," the old woman said, shaking her head.

"It is probably just a matter of Master Parker's lessons," Thomasina answered, heartened by the woman's concern. She acknowledged the curtsy the old woman always insisted upon giving her and wondered what her aunt would say if she knew how Nanny sometimes carried on. The thought of it took her smilingly through the halls until she came to the door of Lady Augusta's sitting room.

The door opened just as she raised her hand to knock, and she had to step aside quickly to avoid being bumped into by Dianna.

"It's about time you came," her cousin snapped, imitating Lady Buckley's abusive style.

"Dianna, enough. Do as I have told you," ordered Lady Augusta's voice. "Enter, Thomasina."

Appearing before her aunt always called to mind a description her mother had oft told her of a governess her mother had had to endure as a young girl at Buckley House. "She looked like she ate lemons at every meal," her mother had said. "Sour and dour as ever a woman was made. Thin as a barren spindle and just as unattractive, but what power she had to make one feel smaller than the tiniest insect—and just as useful."

"Thomasina, your handling of Parker must be firmer in the future, especially during Lord Longeton's stay. He is here to offer for Dianna's hand, and that is of as great an import to your future as to Dianna and all of us," Lady Augusta said with self-confirmed assurance.

"But what can you mean, my lady?" Thomasina asked, becoming suspicious.

"Dianna will need a companion after her marriage and of course, a governess as time passes," the Baroness stated, certain of Thomasina's gratitude. "The benefits of such a position in the Marquess of Thornhill's house should be clear, even to one of your upbringing."

Thomasina dug her nails into her palms. Horror at being trapped into a lifetime of service to Dianna and the Marquess overcame her urge to respond to her aunt's last words.

"You are not to take Parker out—not for a walk nor for your usual ride. Restrict yourselves to the schoolroom and the other rooms of that floor until I give further word."

"But, Aunt—" began Thomasina.

"I will not tell you again, you impertinent child. You are not to be so informal in your address of my person and one in your position learns to hold her tongue." Lady Augusta's voice rose even higher in anger.

"I am sorry, your ladyship," Thomasina forced herself to say. "It is just that Parker will become dreadfully restless if. . . ."

"You will see that he does not," Lady Augusta said in dismissal.

Sighing inwardly, Thomasina curtsied and withdrew. She would have to find a way to deal with Parker's energy indoors—a task that had proven hopeless in the months already spent at Buckley House.

I must not ask for too much, she told herself. *It is clear my aunt will prevent his lordship from even meeting me.* As for Parker, well . . . the assurance of no further contact with "Lord Brutus" would have to suffice for this day's blessings.

Thomasina suddenly realized that this last thought saddened her and, giving herself a vigourous shake, she attacked the problem of how to deal with Parker.

CHAPTER 5

"Dianna, show his lordship the rose garden," Lady Augusta lightly ordered her daughter with an iron undertone.

The girl threw Longeton such a startled look, he took pity. "I would be pleased if you would, Miss Buckley," he said, lightening his frown and offering his arm.

Laying her hand cautiously on it, Dianna threw a petrified plea at her mother.

"Go on now," said Lady Augusta with eyes that belied her airy tone. Dianna dared do naught but lead on.

The trembling of the hand upon his arm could not be caused by the coolness of the air, Longeton decided and spoke, hoping to calm her nerves, and elicit a response that would accredit his decision in a bride. "Your gardens are delightful."

"Yes, your lordship. Mother insists upon the best," answered Dianna, too fearful to look at the sombre-visaged Marquess. "She oversees all the work—of course, much of the original gardens have been removed."

"And what has been your contribution to the scheme?" Longeton asked as he looked about absentmindedly, wishing he knew what had possessed him in coming here.

"I am not allowed . . . that is, I have been away at school until recently," Dianna answered, badly flustered.

"Of course. Your mother has mentioned that," he replied in a quick, offhand manner, the thought suddenly occurring to him that a young boy must be allowed out for fresh air and that his governess would have to escort him.

If it had not been for the Marquess's tone, Dianna would have taken his words for insult since her mother had spoken of her schooling and little else this morn. Stealing a look at his lordship, she was puzzled, for it appeared to her that he was searching the gardens for something or someone.

Longeton, glancing down, caught Dianna's curious stare. Moving his eyes quickly ahead, he saw a tall tightly trimmed hedgerow. "Is that a maze?" he asked.

Taking her eyes from his face, Dianna looked to the hedge. "Why, yes. 'Buckley's Folly' mother calls it. It is the only portion of the gardens that remains from my father's boyhood. For some reason he steadfastly refused to allow it to be torn out. But come, mother said you were to see the rose garden and it is through the trellised portal just ahead."

As they stepped forward, the faint call of a horn drifted overhead.

"What an odd call," noted Longeton. "It cannot be a mail coach."

"Oh heavens, no," Dianna said with feigned horror. "Mother would not allow such an intrusion."

The child is not a complete idiot after all if she realizes her mother is not perfect, thought Longeton as they proceeded into the rose garden. Here he found something to truly admire for it was magnificent, having an array of roses that rivaled those of his estate.

The horn sounded closer. Dianna paused and looked back to the trellis. "It is those Sherrad boys," she said, adopting her mother's haughty demeanour.

Wincing at the nasal tone of her voice, Longeton recalled what the Baron had said of their ages and wondered at her evident dislike.

"Ever since Mathew Sherrad learned that Parker had an enthusiasm for horns, he has sounded a call whenever he approaches Buckley House—childish in the extreme, don't you agree, your lordship? Children should not be encouraged in such silliness," she ended sharply.

Her sullen expression hinted more of exasperation than abhorrence of young Sherrad's entertainment of her brother, the Marquess noted, and decided feminine company of this nature should be taken only in small doses. "If visitors have arrived, we should rejoin your mother," he suggested.

"Lord Sherrad's sons are *not* company,"

Dianna said rebelliously. "Mother will be displeased if we rush."

"As you wish, Miss Buckley," Longeton said but led forward at a more brisk pace. *How,* he thought once again, *did I ever delude myself in thinking I could come to bear being lead about by a green girl of eight and ten whose only words are those "mother said"? Perhaps I should ask Gram if we Longetons are addlepated.* The thought of Gram brought back once more the brooding cast to his features.

Very quickly Dianna was tired by his lordship's pace and agreed they should return to the others. Although she had kept her hand only lightly on his sleeve as they walked, as they neared her mother, who had been joined by the Baron and two passably handsome young gentlemen, Dianna took in a sharp breath and slipped her hand about his arm.

The shorter of the two visitors threw a comradely "hello" to Dianna as they approached while the other stood frowning deeply, his eyes upon Dianna's hand and the Marquess's arm.

Seeing her daughter's hand about his lordship's arm caused Lady Augusta to visibly preen. The Baron turned as he observed his wife's overly pleased behaviour.

"Longeton, these are Lord Sherrad's sons—Viscount Mathew and his brother, Nicholas."

The older Sherrad nodded with barely concealed hostility while Nicholas reached out to shake Longeton's hand.

"Baron Buckley has told us you wish a turn on the hunters," Nicholas said enthusiastically. "Is the roan we saw saddled beside the Baron's Swiftwing yours?"

"Yes. I wish to show his mettle to Baron Buckley before I try his."

"It is a capital beast you have, isn't it Matt?" he said, turning to his brother.

"It looked sound," the young Viscount said, dismissing the subject, his eyes upon Dianna's hand, which still rested upon his lordship's arm. "I did not see Toby or Grandee saddled. Is Thomasina or Parker ill today?" he asked the Baron.

"Ill, ah . . ." stumbled the Baron.

"Neither is ill," Lady Augusta said, rising sharply. "Come, Dianna, the gentlemen wish to be off—unhindered by anyone of our mean."

"Pardon, Lady Augusta," Mathew Sherrad said, bowing to her, "you know that is most untrue. Why, we would welcome the company of two such charming ladies as yourselves. Be convinced to join us."

"Yes, Dianna—as you did before you went to that school," put in Nicholas.

"If you will excuse us," Lady Augusta said with a brisk nod at Dianna, "we must go. Now, daughter." Taking the girl's free hand, she led her towards the house.

"Hrruuumph," the Baron sounded, clearing his throat to attract his visitors' attention. "It appears we must be satisfied with ourselves. No matter, let us be off."

"Why are Tommi and Parker not coming with us?" Mathew asked. "Did someone object?"

"Now, now, calm yourself. Of course no one objected," blustered the Baron. "It is just that, well, my . . . Lady Augusta feels it best if Parker remain indoors today." A bright smile lit the Baron's face. "Yes, that is it. The boy has a touch of a chill. Enough—come along. Swiftwing will outpace all your mounts—despite the extra weight he carries," the Baron challenged with a hearty laugh.

* * *

Hard galloping around the Baron's estate did little to improve Viscount Sherrad's demeanour, and Marquess Longeton looked more dour than ever when they reined to a halt before Buckley House. After a few attempts at conversation at the beginning of the ride, the Baron had taken to setting a fast pace as a solution to the void the attempts caused. Only Nicholas continued to enjoy himself.

Buckley led the way up the steps and through the doors held open by Gill, then on to the main salon. There he went straight to the liquor decanters and poured drinks for everyone.

In silence the glasses were raised, tipped slightly in salute, and emptied. A loud hiccup broke the uneasy stillness. The four glanced at each other, then towards a large, cloth-covered table several feet away. As they stared at the slowly swaying floor-length cloth covering, a strangled hiccup came from its direction.

"Did you say Parker had taken a chill, Lord Buckley?" Nicholas asked, handing his glass to the Baron. "What a shame he could not come on the ride. Swiftwing had not a chance against . . . what was it you called your mount, Lord Longeton?"

"Rapscallion," Longeton replied, "for as a colt he was very mischievous. I almost despaired of his being trained to a useful purpose."

"Exactly as I feel," the Baron said, shaking his head tiredly. "What course did you finally find effective?" he asked, approaching the table as yet another squeak came forth. "Perhaps your trainer could help me with a particular case I have in mind." With these words, he twitched the tablecloth up. "Come out, Parker," he ordered. "You are the only member of this household addled enough to hide in such a place."

A low chuckle from Nicholas caused the Baron to glance at his three guests. Nicholas was striving to forestall a guffaw, and Mathew stood with an expression of commisserate embarrassment upon his features. Even Lord Longeton's usually sombre visage was showing signs of a smile threatening to spread across it. Baffled at the cause of such a reaction to his son caught in such simple mischief, the Baron stepped back to peer under the table.

The hand that had secured his silence at last dropping away, Parker called to Nicholas from under the table, "Is it truly such a fast beast?" unaware that his father had begun to gape.

"Thomasina! What . . . ?"

Voices coming from the hall outside the salon extinguished the Baron's remaining words.

With lightning swiftness, Mathew Sherrad moved forward and pulled the tablecloth in place.

"We did not realize you gentlemen had returned," Lady Augusta piped in false surprise as she minced into the room, Dianna in tow. "Did I hear someone call Thomasina?"

The awkward silence caused by her question was covered by Longeton, who simply ignored it. "How could anyone wish to be from your gracious presence? We rushed to rejoin you."

"You are far too kind, your lordship," she gushed but tossed a questioning glance at her husband, who shrugged slightly in reply. "Well," she said, sweeping the room with a hawkish glance, "I have ordered a cold collation to be served. Would you care to join us?"

"Yes. All of us have a healthy appetite," the Marquess answered. "Baron?"

"Yes, yes. Let us go, by all means. Nothing like a good hard ride to raise an appetite, you know. By all means we will join you, Augusta," he said with obvious relief, herding the Viscount and his brother forward.

"There is no need to rush," Lady Augusta reprimanded her husband, her suspicions raised by his behaviour. "Lord Longeton, you may take Dianna to the dining room and Mathew, you may escort me. What fine young men you and Nicholas have become," she prattled as she searched the room once more for a telltale sign of something amiss.

Longeton briskly led the way from the room. Lady Augusta was forced to fast steps as the young Viscount kept to the pace.

"I would not have thought you so famished," she complained exasperatedly as they left the salon, keeping step for fear of being trod upon by the Baron and Nicholas, who followed heavy on their heels.

Beneath the cloth-covered table, Parker laid his small hand upon Thomasina's in a silent plea for forgiveness. The answering anger in her eyes startled him for they had more than once shared common mirth at being rescued from the fury of Lady Augusta through the efforts of the Sherrad brothers.

"But we were not found out—at least not too badly," he began in protest, falling silent as Thomasina turned her face away. She motioned and he scrambled from beneath the table, holding the cloth up as she followed.

Rising, she smoothed her skirts and, taking Parker by the hand, pulled him along as she went to the door of the salon. Her reserved haughtiness was dropped as she peered around the door.

With a finger raised in caution to Parker, Thomasina dropped his hand and picked up her skirts. After one last survey of the hall, she nodded to Parker and they both burst from the salon and sped down the hall in the opposite direction from the dining room.

CHAPTER 6

The atmosphere lightened as the Buckleys and their guests enjoyed the cold repast. Viscount Sherrad's demeanour towards Longeton softened; knowledge of a shared secret caused the conversation to flow much more freely than it had.

"Is it true we shall have music after we dine on the morrow?" Nicholas asked Lady Augusta.

"Yes. The musicians are coming from London and . . . I have sent further invitations. There shall be more young people. It will be quite an evening for Buckley House," she answered, preening.

Longeton lost the trend of conversation as he recalled the sight of Thomasina huddled beneath the table trying to hang onto the boy. *Certainly a different manner of chit than usual*, he thought with an inward smile. It would be most interesting to have an opportunity to speak with her.

"I am happy you are pleased, your lordship."

Lady Augusta's words broke through his ruminations. He nodded affably, disguising his lack of attention.

"Of course, you will lead Dianna out for the first set," Lady Augusta continued with certainty.

Comprehension dawned upon the Marquess and his wits scrambled to save him. "But I cannot," he said smoothly.

"But why?" retorted the ruffled Baroness.

"It is only fitting that I should lead out only the most gracious lady present first," he answered with a slight twitch of his brow, "and of course, my lady, that can only be you."

The Baroness's ego ballooned at this flattery.

"But of course, for you I will dance with all the ladies of your most pleasant household," Longeton added, nodding graciously at Dianna.

Lady Augusta's self-satisfaction dispelled any suspicion of his intent.

"That means that Thomasina will be present for the dance then, does it not?" asked Mathew Sherrad, seeing the opening Longeton had presented.

"Why . . . why . . ." stumbled the flustered Lady Augusta.

"Thomasina, ah, yes, your niece, I believe," the Marquess said casually. Pausing, he looked questioningly at the Baroness. "There is some reason why she should not be allowed to be present?" he asked with just a tinge of suspicion in his voice.

Glowering first at the Viscount, Lady Augusta swung a weak smile to the Marquess. "Of course not," she said. "It is just that Thomasina has not, well . . . has not moved in a very large social circle. She has just come out of mourning and I did not want to make her feel . . . any distress."

The questioning scowl deepened upon Longeton's features.

"But she will be persuaded to join us," the Baroness rushed on, deciding there was more harm in making his lordship suspicious than in having the ungrateful girl present. The thought of presenting Thomasina at so large a gathering rankled, but she soothed her distaste with the knowledge that Thomasina's presence would be eclipsed by her own triumph. This was to be her victory over all her neighbors and their daughters. Everyone would have to know that Lord Longeton was present for only one reason, and if they did not she would be certain the fault was corrected.

Lady Augusta looked at Dianna with unaccustomed fondness only to change to frowning as she saw her daughter huddled over her plate, not daring to look at the Marquess. Longeton, himself, was looking more pleased than at any time since his arrival, she noted with pleasure. But men are unpredictable, was her reasoning. She would have to see that Buckley got the matter settled—the sooner the better for all.

Upstairs, having returned safely to the schoolroom, Thomasina was giving Parker a sound scolding.

He stood before her, head dropped, lip protruding, slowly shuffling his feet.

"But we always go riding with Matt and Nicholas," he protested as she ended. "It is not fair we should have to stay here just because *he* is here."

"It might not be fair, Parker, but it is what we have been told to do, and you must learn the virtue of obedience. Your lack of it will cause my death yet. If your mother had discovered us, you would have a tutor tomorrow and I would be sent away. There can be no more pranks."

"But, Tommi—"

"No, Parker. For both of our welfares, you must behave properly. Do you wish to see me gone?"

"No, Tommi, you know I do not, but. . . ."

Thomasina shook her head. "Your mother has her mind set upon this match for Dianna. She will not hesitate to be done with anyone she views as a danger to it—"

". . . and I may be a danger to it," finished

Parker sadly. "Why don't they love me, Tommi? *Am* I so bad?"

"They do love you, Parker," she answered softly, struck by his sudden grief. "It is that they have trouble showing it," she added, hugging him to her.

"Oh, Tommi," he choked out through silent tears, "can you not marry the Marquess and take me away with you? I would never misbehave again, ever."

With a harsh, choked laugh pushed from her throat, Thomasina took Parker by the shoulders. Her eyes looked directly into his as she said forcefully, "Your parents love you very much—you are not to think otherwise, no matter how it seems to you. You must never say—never even think—such a thought again. Do you understand?"

Parker nodded—the telltale sign of mischief suddenly twinkling to the fore in his eyes.

Thomasina saw it, and compassion for the boy fled. "To our books, Master Buckley," she ordered sternly, "and this time you sit on the side opposite the door. Let us review your geography lesson. Name the sovereign countries on the continent."

Taking his seat complacently, Parker began the list. "France, under the rule of His Royal Highness, Louis XVIII. . . ."

Neither her eyes saw nor her ears heard his answers as Thomasina mulled over his previous words. *Whatever comes upon children's minds*? she thought. *How could he ever have gotten that idea? I and "Lord Brutus"? The poor child needs lessons in what is required of the rescuers of damsels in distress!*

Thomasina forced her mind from the subject and to listen to Parker, but part of it asked, Could not "Lord Brutus" fulfill some of those requirements?

CHAPTER 7

The entire household was in a flurry of activity. Although the invited guests for the evening's entertainment were not large enough in number to be able to term the event a "ball" it would be a very large soiree.

Lisa, who usually found cause to dawdle and visit whenever she came to the schoolroom, merely set the breakfast tray upon the table, rolled her eyes, and left.

Thomasina ate heartily, bracing herself for the day, as Parker was already showing signs of restlessness. If only there were some way he could have a romp out-of-doors, she thought, but she dared not ask her Aunt Augusta. *Not today, even though I would like to see more than these four walls.* A glance at Parker, shifting uneasily in his chair as he idly stirred his porridge, caused her to mentally calculate the risks of venturing forth without asking permission. This done, she reached a quick decision.

"Parker, have Nanny help you change to your riding boots. I will be but a moment in changing into my riding habit."

"But you said—"

"I cannot see the harm in our going for a short ride this early in the morn. No one can be stirring but Mr. Gill and Mrs. Brown, with all the servants. We can trust the grooms not to betray us. Do you not want to go?"

In answer, Parker scooted off his chair, ran and hugged her. "I was dreadful afraid you had changed, Tommi," he said. "Let us race to see who is ready first."

Both scrambled to their rooms, Parker emerging first. He grinned triumphantly as Thomasina joined him. Returning the smile, she took his hand and made for the end of the floor and the servants' stairs.

The few who saw them paid no mind, being accustomed to their odd comings and goings.

"Good morn to ye, miss, and to ye, Master Parker," Bently greeted them. "I take it ye be wantin' Toby and Grandee?"

Thomasina acknowledged his greeting and nodded to his question. "How is your wife?" she asked him after he had signaled an undergroom to saddle their mounts.

"She be much improved, than's to ye, miss. The poultice has much improved the looks o' the leg."

"I regret I have not been able to stop in."

"It be understood, miss. We than' ye for what ye 'ave done. Ah, here be the mounts." Bently lifted Parker easily into the saddle. Turning to Grandee, he checked the cinch, then lifted Thomasina into the sidesaddle.

Settling into it and arranging her skirts, Thomasina spoke slowly, "I am afraid, Bently, that no one knows—"

"Then best ye keep to the unused paths," he laughed, cutting her off. "And come back by way of the path back of the stables. Now off with ye—do not tarry too long." He watched as she and Parker rode away. "A fine lass, that one be," he said to the undergroom. "Too bad his lordship don't . . . ah, well, best to be back to work. We'll 'ave many an extra to find a place for this eve. Back to work with ye."

Once out of sight of the main house and its surrounding buildings, Thomasina picked up the pace. Grandee was restless from not having been ridden and was anxious for the outing. Toby, as always, had to be prodded forward. Thomasina gave Grandee her head since they rode this way often enough for her to know the path, and Parker would know where she would halt and await him.

The wind swept across her face, exhilarating her, and she urged the mare to an even faster stride. The path they traveled was narrow and hemmed by shrubbery on both sides and the pace dangerous, for Thomasina had ridden little before coming to Buckley House. Since her arrival she had acquired a fair seat and generally was careful, but she did not have the judgment of a seasoned rider. This morn the judgment she did have was tossed aside as she felt the need to be completely unfettered—to forget the disarray of her emotions. Thus she rocketed down the narrow, little-used path, unheedful of everything.

A large roan appeared just as her ears discerned the sound of approaching hooves. The path was too narrow at this point for them to pass safely. Pulling frantically on the reins, the last thing Thomasina saw was a pair of startled, angry, emerald-green eyes.

Parker, who had been forced to follow at a slower pace due to Toby's sluggishness, was not witness to the mishap but only heard the frantic neighing and crashing sounds. Thumping his heels against Toby's sides, he urged the pony down the path. Fear grabbed at him as he saw Grandee coming towards him, her saddle empty. The mare stopped as she approached her constant companion and Parker drew Toby to a halt. Sliding to the ground, he grabbed Grandee's reins and secured both mounts to a nearby branch. Racing down the path, he ran with a pace akin to the rapid beat of his heart.

The sight of a large roan hobbling towards him slowed his stride. Approaching the steed slowly, he clutched the reins as the stallion snorted and tossed his head but allowed the boy to hold him.

"Why, you are his lordship's steed," Parker said as he patted the animal and looked at the right foreleg, which the animal was holding from the ground. "It doesn't look too bad, boy," he said, tying the steed to a low branch. "I'll be back as soon as I can." Sprinting away, Parker rounded the next turn of the path. Before him lay Thomasina, Lord Longeton bent over her.

"Tommi!" he screamed, making a running leap and plopping down at her side.

Thomasina lay upon her back, eyes closed, breathing very shallowly, unnaturally pale.

"She's dead." Parker sought denial from the Marquess.

"Calm yourself. She is not dead and will not be so for some time to come. Struck her head when she fell from the saddle. I can feel no broken bones. Here," he ordered, handing Parker a kerchief. "Wet it with the dew from the grass and bring it back—at once!"

Parker scurried to do as he was told, never questioning the command in his thankfulness that Thomasina was not seriously harmed.

When he returned to their side, he found the Marquess sitting upon the ground, holding Thomasina across his lap with one arm about her. With his free hand he was loosening the top buttons of her riding habit.

"What are you gawking at boy?" Longeton snapped, taking the dampened kerchief. Gently he wiped Thomasina's face and then placed it across her brow, nodding with satisfaction to himself. Glancing up, he encountered Parker's open-mouthed stare.

"You must be Master Parker," he said easily. "I am Brutus Longeton. Did you see Rapscallion as you were coming?"

"Raps . . . Rapscallion?"

Longeton laughed. "A large roan—" He ended his words abruptly as Thomasina stirred.

"Yes, sir . . . your lordship. I tethered him just beyond the curve. He's favouring his right foreleg, but it doesn't look to be too bad."

"Good," the Marquess answered, shifting his attention back to the boy. "Does Miss Thait always ride like the devil had found her?"

"No, sir . . . your lordship, that is. Tommi has a good seat—she's always telling me to be careful. It's only that she's not been herself since. . . ." His voice trailed off guiltily.

"Since you pushed her out of the tree?" Longeton asked.

Parker nodded unhappily.

"You must treat Miss Thait more carefully in the future. She could have been seriously injured in such a fall. What if she would have not held to the vine—or it had broken? Or if she had gone into hysterics when all was done?" Longeton scolded lightly.

Wide-eyed, Parker said, "I never thought the vine might break, but Tommi would never let go—not her. And she would never go into a fright," he finished confidently.

A moan came from Thomasina.

"Everything is all right, Tommi," Longeton said quietly. "Lie still now."

Relaxing, she did as he said.

"Wait a while longer, then open your eyes slowly," she heard the soft, kindly voice say.

Returning to a grasping awareness, Thomasina did as the voice suggested. Slowly her vision focused on the face above hers. Recognition came and she attempted to sit up abruptly, but a terrible pounding in her head caused her to lean back involuntarily into the comforting security of his arm. She rested her head momentarily upon his chest and felt the ripple of muscle in his arm beneath her back. Hesitantly, she raised her head until their eyes met and each was held by the other's.

"Are you all right?" insisted Parker, placing his hand upon her arm. "Tommi, speak to me."

Mesmerized by the cool green pools she was gazing into, she answered with a vague "yes." Turning her head towards Parker, she stared at him; then full comprehension returned.

"Parker? What happened? Where is Grandee? Is she unhurt? What happened to the fool who. . . ." Her staccato questions ended as she looked at the Marquess once more.

"You!" she said accusingly.

"Is it such a crime to be myself?" Longeton asked, regaining some of his reserve.

Thomasina had become rigid in his arms. "The question needs no answer," she snapped. "If you will please unhand me."

"You appear normal enough. Parker, give Miss Thait your hand and help her rise."

Taking it, Thomasina stood unsteadily. She

would have fallen had not Longeton sprang up and supported her.

"You have no sense, do you?" he scolded. "Let me help you be seated," he urged.

"No—I am only a bit light-headed." She took the kerchief Parker had picked up and now held out to her. Lightly patting her face, she said, "I am much improved now. You may release me—please."

Longeton stepped back, his scowl once more firmly in place. Fine spirit but little enough sense, he thought. Most women would be having a fit of hysteria and none would have objected to my aid. What was the cause of her intense dislike?

"I apologize, Lord Longeton," Thomasina said shakily. "I should not have been riding on this path at such a reprehensible speed. I trust you were not injured?"

"He's fine," piped in Parker, "but his roan has an injured foreleg."

"I . . . I am sorry . . . for the animal, your lordship," she said. Then thinking once more of her mother, she turned away. "Grandee and Toby?" she asked Parker.

"They are unhurt. Just down the path where I left them," he answered.

Thomasina stepped forward unsteadily.

"Let me assist you—you have taken a rather nasty fall," Longeton insisted, once more stepping closer.

"No." Two brown eyes sparkled angrily at him.

Shrugging, Longeton motioned Parker to her side. In silence the pair shuffled forward, the Marquess staying close to Thomasina's other side, ready to aid her if necessary.

When they reached the animals, Thomasina realized there was only one way for her to reach her saddle. "If you please, your lordship," she said grudgingly.

Longeton stepped before her. Taking her waist in his hands, he said in an undertone, "It will please me greatly," and lifted her into the saddle. His hands lingered for an odd moment, but looking into his eyes Thomasina felt no desire to reprove him. He lowered his hands, took hold of Grandee's reins, and handed them to her. "Are you certain you will be able to ride?"

"Yes, of course. But . . . no one knows we are out this morn. . . ."

"You need not fear my telling." He turned and put Parker in his saddle. "Lead the way to the stables slowly for Miss Thait," he commanded, "and see that she is allowed to rest the remainder of the day."

"Yes, sir," Parker answered snappily, beaming with a bright smile.

Longeton released Grandee and led Toby forward a short distance. "Can you come to my rooms without being seen?" he asked the boy conspiratorially.

Parker nodded eagerly.

"Come to them after you sup."

Saluting sharply, Parker then looked back and saw Thomasina urging Grandee forward. The mare, no longer frisky after her fall, went obediently.

"I will send a groom for you, Lord Longeton," Thomasina said primly.

"That will not be necessary. It would be best if I made my way back alone. And," a slight smile clouded his scowl as he hesitated, "you had better redo the buttons on your bodice before you reach the stables."

Thomasina's eyes swiftly followed his gaze and she gasped. Her free hand clasped her collars together. Blushing fiercely and without another look at the Marquess, she urged Grandee on, halting only when out of his sight. With a shaking hand she fastened the buttons and then smoothed her hair. Against her will, the feeling of security she had experienced before she realized whose arm held her returned. A tear wended its way down her cheek.

Oh, mother, her heart cried. *The despicable man can only remind me to do my buttons, and that after all he has done to us!* Another tear followed the first.

Looking back, Parker saw the tears. "Does your head hurt so terribly, Tommi?" he asked with concern. "I will be good all day for Nanny so you may rest. Then you will feel much better," he concluded assuredly.

Thomasina wiped the remains of the two tears away with the kerchief in her hand. Looking at it, she saw the crest, carefully embroidered on it, and realized whose it was. Her hand crumpled it into a ball. Raising her hand to toss it away, she found the action stayed by another tear. After dabbing it away, she tucked the kerchief into her sleeve cuff and urged Grandee forward.

CHAPTER 8

Light pierced the gloom of night triumphantly from all the windows and doors of Buckley House. Decorative lanterns twinkled gaily about the gardens outside the ballroom, providing soft glows in contrast to the brilliant shafts of light blazing forth from the trio of double doors that faced the gardens and were opened to allow the cooler evening air to enter and also to provide a convenient exit for those who sought the evening breeze or wished to stroll along the more dimly lit trimmed paths.

Looking to the front of Buckley House, one could see an ever increasing mélange of carriages and finely matched pairs as guests continued to arrive in steady numbers.

Lady Augusta had never presided over a receiving line with such gloating satisfaction. It seemed all those invited were making an appearance.

No one would ever dare to snub her again, she thought as she smiled and nodded repeatedly, greeting all with smugness; they had not always been so willing to attend her house.

Dianna stood at her mother's side, a faint echo of the other. Her gown of white satin became her sparse frame and roses from the gardens improved her coffee-coloured hair, which had been done in the latest style. Only the heads of the more elderly guests were adorned with periwigs and perukes. Lady Augusta had been very relieved when Lord Longeton had appeared at supper with none. Pride in knowing the proper form had induced her to try several of her own on Dianna, but they succeeded only in making the girl a ridiculous figure—an oversize puff of white atop a rail-thin stick. The desire to create a pleasing impression overcame that to follow the proper style.

Dianna's pale smile was a sallow shadow of her mother's overbearing, gloating one. She dared to steal a glance at Lord Longeton, whom Lady Augusta had maneuvered to place at her side at the last moment. His usual sombre face appeared hollow-cheeked and sinister to the young girl as his brooding scowl grew deeper with each lifted eyebrow of those who passed through the line. The Marquess was a forbidding person to her and his presence was having an ever increasing disquieting effect upon her. All her mother's fine words upon the advantages of a match with his lordship were losing their glow.

A look at her mother's supremely self-satisfied face assured Dianna that chance of escaping the match if his lordship persisted would be nonexistent. For an instant a look of dismay covered her weak smile.

Longeton chanced to glance down at that moment and wondered briefly at its cause. As his eyes met hers, she bit her lip and ducked her head. Instantly, he thought of another pair of eyes—far more lively and definitely more challenging. Longeton realized he would have preferred those eyes to be beside him now.

Time drifted slowly for the Marquess, who had found receiving lines a scourge since coming to the title. His usual demeanour concealed this, concealed all of his emotions. Those he came in contact with, socially or through business, judged him a hard man, completely noncommital as far as personal feelings were concerned. Only those who had grown up with him and known him intimately in the years before the title was forced upon him thought his present bearing odd—changed—and regretted it. They would have recognized the Marquess far more easily if they had seen his visit with Parker that same afternoon rather than as he now stood in the receiving line.

Parker's enthusiasm for the Marquess had become boundless since the morning's incident. Only Mathew Sherrad and Thomasina had treated the boy with any kindness in his brief dealings with adults. Longeton acted as if he were an adult and Parker accepted the responsibility robustly—Thomasina would have rested the day away even had she not desired to! It was an eager lad who had stolen to the rooms Longeton occupied after bolting down his supper.

Seeing much of himself in the young boy, Longeton treated the lad as if he were a man. Parker responded with admiration and loyalty. Without realizing it, he had answered the Marquess's unasked questions. Both were pleased when their chat ended.

The stream of incoming guests had slowed to a trickle; at last the signal was given for the receiving line to end. Longeton offered his arm to Lady Augusta and led the way to the ballroom. Their entrance caused the musicians to strike the first notes. With a flourish, the Marquess led the Baroness through the first minuet, the other guests gradually joining them.

To all who observed him, Longeton's deportment showed only disinterest. In truth, however, his eyes swept over the guests, searching.

At the end of the minuet he gave Lady Augusta a gracious bow and went to claim his dance with Dianna. Walking towards her, he saw to one side that Viscount Sherrad was entering from the garden and upon his arm was Thomasina.

Dianna quaked at the Marquess's fierce scowl as he bowed and offered his arm to lead the next country set. Not a word was exchanged the entire dance as both members of the pair watched a fellow pair with hidden interest.

Longeton observed that Thomasina moved somewhat stiffly, as would be expected after her fall that morn, and also that she made her steps uncertainly as would one who had seldom danced. He noted also that she cast an ever grateful smile at Mathew Sherrad. The attentiveness with which the Viscount showered his companion was also noticed by Dianna. . .

The set ended; Longeton bowed to Dianna. Curtsying in return, she rose and took his arm. Together they wended their way through the milling dancers, halting before Sherrad and Thomasina.

"I have given my word that I would dance with all the ladies of this household," Longeton said smoothly. "Miss Thait?"

With an anxious look to Mathew, who

nodded, Thomasina raised her eyes to Longeton's defiantly.

"If you will pardon me, my lord," she said with equal aplomb, "I would rather—"

"There you are," piped Lady Augusta's shrill voice, interrupting Thomasina.

With a brief bow to the Baroness, Longeton said, "There is no need to search me out, my lady. I am willingly carrying out my promise to dance with all members of your household. Miss Thait and I were about to join the next set, were we not?"

The realization that she had been outmanuevered without a word spoken on her part rendered Lady Augusta speechless.

"I will decline if you wish, Aunt," Thomasina said.

"You will do no such thing, young woman," Lady Augusta scolded. "Unless his lordship wishes to withdraw his most gracious offer to such an ungrateful child," she ended, looking hopefully at the Marquess.

The music had begun and Longeton answered by holding out his hand. Thomasina dared do nothing but place her hand in his.

Mathew offered his arm to Dianna and the foursome joined the dance.

Lady Augusta watched them pensively, then relaxed as it was apparent that both Thomasina and Dianna were not speaking to their escorts. "At least the chit knows her place," she said under her breath. Spying her husband, the Baroness set sail, preparing to broadside him. "Where have you been? Well, no matter. Have you managed to speak with his lordship privately about the matter? Speak up. What have you to say?"

"Now, my dear . . ." began the Baron.

"So, you have failed, as usual. Must I attend to all matters?" she demanded.

"It would be most unseemly for you to approach his lordship about this matter," answered her husband with a slight show of spirit.

Forcing a smile to replace her grimace as she saw guests approaching them, Lady Augusta whispered to her husband. "I want this matter settled—this eve. . . . Why Lady Penelope, how kind of you and Lord Audley to come," she greeted the couple before them.

On the dance floor, two gentlemen were feeling the chill of disfavour. In one it raised an unusual wry humour, in the other, further dismay. Neither man had chance for words, the steps of the set being intricate and their partners claimed by others as soon as the last note fell silent.

Towards the end of the first hour of dancing, Thomasina was once more claimed for a dance by Viscount Sherrad. He had seen that his acquaintances kept Thomasina constantly upon the floor.

"Mathew, could we please not join them?" Thomasina asked as they approached the pairs forming for a country set.

Sherrad's eyes narrowed in concern. "If that is what you wish. Not up to all the excitement, eh?" he teased her.

"I am a bit thirsty and certainly somewhat worn down."

Gazing at her apologetically, the Viscount said, "I had forgotten how tiring dancing can be—counting and watching all those steps and turns." He smiled encouragingly.

With a laugh Thomasina agreed. "I have trounced enough feet this evening to ensure my abandonment."

"No, you could never be abandoned, Thomasina," Mathew said sincerely, then his mood shifted. "I tell you what—you step outdoors. I shall fetch an ice and join you. There is a matter I would like to discuss with you."

Her eyes quizzed him.

"I shall say no more," he laughed. "Go out—I shall not be long. If anyone should ask you to dance, tell him I have spoken for you."

Thomasina watched him weave his way through the crowd, a half-smile upon her lips, then turned and exited through the first set of doors she came to. The cool night breeze fanned her gently. With a heavy sigh she moved to a semisecluded corner of the dimly lit garden and indulged in a very unladylike stretch. Sore from her fall, she knew morning would cause her to feel the results of the night's dancing even more. Another long sigh escaped as she seated herself on a nearby bench. From it she could watch for Mathew.

What could he wish to discuss? she wondered. All was forgotten as she heard, "Miss Thait," said quietly behind her.

Rising sharply, she spun around awkwardly to confront the Marquess.

"I see you, too, felt the need for relief from the exertions of the dance," Longeton said as he stepped around the bench. "Do you think it wise to be so active after such a fall as this morn's?" he asked, taking in her moon-haloed stance.

"It is no concern of yours, my lord," Thomasina snapped, her eyes surveying his strong jawline, firm lips, and broad shoulders, even as her mind struggled against the impression. "Mathew . . . Viscount Sherrad is to join me, so if you please. . . ."

An eyebrow twitched sardonically, "I see."

His tone raised Thomasina's ire. "If you will not go, I shall," she said angrily, turning away only to feel the strong grip of his hand upon her wrist. "How dare you," she said, her eyes sparking their outrage.

Longeton's eyes flickered briefly; then a screen covered his emotions. "You are a troublesome chit," he said exasperatedly. "Perhaps my first assessment of you was the correct one." An iron grip drew Thomasina closer. The Marquess raked her face with his gaze, his expression startling her.

"You are hurting my wrist," she gasped, grappling for words to break his spell.

"I have no desire to harm you," he said stonily, "and I shall claim what you have chosen to give Sherrad." With these words his hand pulled her roughly to him, his free arm encircling her waist as his lips claimed hers in a rough, vexatious kiss. Freeing her lips, he gazed at her still upturned face. The moonlight gleaming off her copper curls added a note of quaintness to her features. With an oath, he released her and strode away.

Nearing the ballroom, he did not acknowledge Sherrad's salute as they passed one another. As he halted and cast about for Thomasina, Mathew wondered what could have caused such a black look. Spying her, he joined her in a few quick strides. "Here is your ice, Tommi. Sip it and you will be instantly revived," he said gaily as he held it out to her.

Thomasina reached for it slowly. Desperation flickered for an instant as she raised her eyes to his.

"Is something wrong, Tommi?" he asked, struck by her forlornness.

"Of course not, Mathew," she answered, taking the ice and seating herself.

Sitting beside her, Sherrad reached for her hand. "I am your friend, Tommi. Tell me what is troubling you. Has one of my friends been too bold?"

"Oh, no," she answered with a forced laugh. "It is . . . it is—well, I took a fall . . . a fall from Grandee this morn." Looking up, she was touched by the concern that crossed his features.

"I was not harmed in any way," she assured him. "Only bruised and now terribly stiff. It was stupid of me to fall."

"And I was making certain you had no dance free," Mathew said with mild disgust. "Why did you not tell me sooner?"

"No one knows of it but . . . Parker."

"Ah, that explains it," he broke in. "I must speak with that young rascal. You are much too lenient with him."

"Now you sound like my aunt," Thomasina retorted.

"The world can survive only one Aunt Augusta," he replied with mock seriousness.

Their mutual laughter mingled with the music and chatter coming from the ballroom.

"That is better, Tommi. I think it would be best if you simply stole away to your room. What I had to speak of can wait. If the

Baroness should ask after you, I shall say you had a headache."

"The ache 'tis far from there," quipped Thomasina and both laughed.

Viscount Sherrad watched her walk back into the ballroom, his mind flitting nimbly about. Longeton's black look and Tommi's disconcertion, plus the other set of odd facts—Thomasina had taken a fall from Grandee and the Marquess's stallion had been injured in a tumble—were the two pairs connected? As he rubbed his chin, a gleam of hope entered his eyes. With a low chuckle, he rejoined the guests in the ballroom.

CHAPTER 9

Fog billowed in large soggy clouds about the grounds of Buckley House. The dreariness of the morning matched Longeton's mood.

Gideon entered quietly. One look at his master vanquished his greeting. Instead he simply held out the silver tray he was carrying.

Longeton glanced from the crested letter upon it to Gideon in wordless question.

"One of your grooms brought it just moments ago, my lord," the valet answered.

With a headshake of resignation Longeton

took it and broke the seal. "Destroy it," he ordered Gideon after a brief reading, dropping it upon the tray and turning back to the window.

Watching while tufts of fog slowly slid by, Longeton contemplated his situation. It had been foolish to promise Gram and even more foolish to go about his selection in the manner he had; most foolish was his letter and journey to Buckley House, he thought. Now that Gram has her teeth sunk into the issue, she will not let go. "Issue." The word echoed in his mind. With a hollow laugh, he turned back to the room. "Issue" was his problem. Gram's note was explicit; he had promised her a betrothal and she wished to know where it was.

Longeton cursed silently. Why had not his brother taken the time to marry and produce a son? Better a guardian than a bridegroom!

Gideon paused in mid-step as he was reentering the room. Perhaps, he thought, seeing his lordship's stance, it would be most strategic to exit at this time.

"Where are you going?" Longeton thundered. "Pack. We are leaving at once—in the coach. Order the groom who brought the missive to bring Rapscallion to Thornhill as soon as the leg improves. He is to use an easy pace. Tell him to travel with care—I want no more harm to come to the stallion."

"Yes, my lord. Will there be anything else?"

"Fetch some writing materials for me."

"Yes, my lord, at once," Gideon answered, bowing as he backed from the room. Matters here had gone awry, he thought, definitely awry.

With a final shrug, the fine cambric jacket slipped over the Marquess's smoothly-muscled shoulders. Parker's reflection in the mirror he faced caused his frown to lighten.

"Well, Master Parker, how do you fare this day?" he asked good-naturedly.

"I am fine, sir, your lordship. But I fear for Tommi," the boy answered worriedly.

"There is no need to fear for her," Longeton scoffed, then regretted his words as Parker's perturbation increased.

"You would not say that if you had heard her cry all night as I did," the boy said angrily.

"All night?"

Lowering his eyes before Longeton's demanding stare, Parker said, "I might have fallen asleep for a short while. But, well, Tommi never cries." His eyes pleaded for belief, for help.

"Women are unpredictable creatures," Longeton said, walking up to the boy and placing an arm comfortingly across his shoulders. "You will learn as much when you gather a few more years. Am I not correct in saying that Miss Thait assured you nothing was troubling her this morn?"

Parker nodded.

"Believe her then. Ah, Gideon, have my orders been carried out?" he asked as the valet entered.

"Yes, my lord."

"Good. You may pack the things in here; I am finished."

Glancing about, Parker asked, "You are leaving?"

Longeton turned from the boyish innocence. "Yes. I received a summons from my grandmother this morn. I must return to Thornhill at once."

"We shall see you again, shan't we?"

"I . . . I do not know. Possibly. You had

better return to the schoolroom before you are missed," he ended brusquely.

"Yes, your lordship," Parker answered hesitantly, then turned and ran from the room as Longeton kept his back turned.

"Your writing material is upon the desk in the other room, my lord," Gideon said quietly.

"What? . . . Oh, yes. See that I am not disturbed. The coach should be ready when I have finished my note. Have the baggage loaded so that we may depart as soon as you hand the message to Gill." Longeton stalked from the room before the valet answered.

Seating himself abruptly, he grabbed the quill, dipped it into the inkwell but was forestalled by the blank page before him. The quill hovered above the paper as a vison of moon-lit copperish curls came to his mind. The thought was angrily dismissed, the pen redipped and words flowed quickly from it.

Longeton emerged from the room with grimness wrapped about him. Wordlessly, the sealed missive was handed to Gideon and in a short time the Marquess was journeying towards Thornhill.

The pale afternoon sun warmed Thomasina's back as she watched Parker frolicking with the head groom's dog. Their confinement had ended shortly after word reached them through Lisa that the Marquess had gone. The news had not brought Thomasina the relief she expected and she quickly buried herself in Parker's lessons.

"You are sour as any old tutor would be," he had complained after Lisa had left their luncheon tray. "*Must* we work all day?"

Relenting, she agreed they could go to the garden as soon as lunch was eaten and the lesson completed. In an attempt to make up for her sternness, Thomasina had sent word for Bently's dog to be brought to the gardens. The boy and dog had been happily bounding about ever since they had been introduced.

"The word is true then," a voice stated flatly behind Thomasina, startling her.

"I did not mean to frighten you," Viscount Sherrad apologized. "May I sit with you?"

Thomasina moved to make room for him. "You did not sound your horn," she said questioningly.

"No, I did not wish to announce my visit. I

was certain you and Parker would be out if Longeton had departed."

A strange look clouded Thomasina's features.

"You are still bothered by your fall?" he asked with concern.

"No"— Thomasina forced a weak laugh—"merely stiff."

There was a brief silence as both watched Parker, who had not noticed the Viscount's presence.

"Why did you not wish your visit announced?" Thomasina quizzed.

A red tinge came to Mathew's cheeks. "I desired to speak with you privately, Tommi," he said very seriously, "and knew that would be impossible with Aunt Augusta about. I told you last eve there was a matter I wished to discuss with you." Rising, the Viscount looked away, searching for the words.

A curdling thought came to Thomasina's mind as she viewed Mathew's blush and the nervous fidgeting of his hands. *He means to ask for my hand,* she thought with dismay. Best to be done with it quickly then, she reasoned. Gulping, she reached out. "What is it,

Mathew?" she asked hoping her voice was steadier than her hand.

Still gazing at the garden, Sherrad's words spewed out. "If I did not feel such affection for you, Tommi, I would not ask this of you. But I have no other to turn to. You must help me. Please say you will!" he pleaded, turning his eyes to meet hers.

"What has upset you so, Mathew? Of course I will do whatever I can," Thomasina assured him with relief. She clapped a hand to her mouth as she felt a gurgle of laughter rise within, but found she could not restrain the impish release.

The Viscount stiffened. "I fail to see what you find humourous in my words," he said, taking offense.

"But you cannot know what I was thinking," she gasped between laughter and giggles. Forcing herself to sober slightly, she continued, "You must think me very missish, even silly, but for a moment I feared you were going to ask for my hand."

"But I was," the Viscount retorted, "and, well, I see no humour in it."

"Neither do I," a very sober Thomasina answered.

"Do not look so, Tommi. Let me explain myself."

"My lord, that, I certainly hope you can do," she said slowly.

Parker tumbled over the dog as he ran back towards Thomasina.

"Matt!" he hooted as he saw the Viscount at her side. Bounding up, he ran to the pair.

"You did not sound your horn," he said accusingly.

"No, but I have only now arrived," Mathew assured the boy. "Shall I take you for a ride upon Thunder?"

"Yes," shouted the boy joyfully, grabbing Mathew's hand and tugging at him to rise.

"What is your answer, Thomasina?" the Viscount asked her as he rose. "Run ahead and have the groom mount you," he told Parker, who scampered off happily.

Thomasina rose and walked with Mathew as they slowly followed the boy.

"What will you say?" he asked again.

"I like it not," she answered, her hesitancy apparent in her voice, "but, for you, I will agree."

Beaming, Mathew halted and bowed to

her. "My deepest gratitude, Miss Thait. I am honoured indeed."

"Mathew!" Parker called back excitedly.

"You had better join him," Thomasina laughed, "before he brings out the entire household."

Taking her hand, to her surprise he kissed it. "You must become accustomed to that," he laughed as he saw her expression. After a bow, he joined Parker.

With a shake of her head, Thomasina sighed and walked slowly to the house.

CHAPTER 10

The Dowager Marchioness of Thornhill's contemplation of the chessboard before her was disturbed by the clatter of hooves and the crunch of coach wheels upon the gravel drive before the mansion.

"Jane," she ordered crisply, "to the window. Is it my grandson?"

The abigail laid aside her work, rose stoicly, and trod heavily to the window of the small salon.

"It is his coach, my lady, but I do not see that stallion his lordship rides," she told the old Marchioness with a familiarity acquired during fifty-odd years of service—first strictly as a lady's maid and then more and more as a companion.

Lady Longeton struggled to her feet. With the aid of a cane she made her way determinedly to the window.

"See, my lady. His lordship is alighting from the coach," Jane said as if to affirm the absence of Rapscallion.

"Wouldn't have believed it—he actually rode in the baggage coach. That black look he bears does not bode well for the betrothal." She watched as Longeton strode up the steps.

"My guess would be the library," Jane said as she went back to her work.

Nodding, the Marchioness turned herself towards the doors. The slam of a door down the hall from them echoed loudly into the salon.

"Correct once more, Jane. That places you ahead. Note the score while I attend to this abrupt return." The still regal figure worked her way to the library.

The thumping cane alerted Longeton to his

grandmother's presence long before her voice did so.

"On the path to dissipation," she observed tonelessly. "I had understood you disliked your brother's habits."

Longeton faced his grandmother. "The doctor said you were not to be up and especially not walking," he stated reprovingly.

"I will decide when I can and cannot walk. His head is filled with too much 'modern' gibberish. But you will not fob me off with this concern. What of your betrothal?" she asked, edging closer.

"There will be none," he said, turning away.

Staring at the broad-shouldered back, the Marchioness opened her mouth to speak; but with age she had acquired some wisdom and thus changed her mind. Instead she laboured to a chair. "I will partake of some brandy with you," she said as she awkwardly sat.

Longeton poured a second glass wordlessly and handed it to his grandmother.

"Sit with me," she ordered. "What occurred to bring you home in the baggage coach?"

With a glowering look, the Marquess sipped his brandy, not answering.

"Have you taken Duard's gambling habit upon yourself, also, then?" she asked tersely. "Has the animal been lost to the gaming table?"

"Rapscallion was slightly injured in a fall. The groom you sent is bringing him home later in easy stages," Longeton said curtly, standing as he finished.

"Where are you going? Seat yourself."

Shrugging, he took his seat once more.

The Marchioness softened her tone. "Was the Buckley wench so unbearable? She was, after all, your own choice."

His hands waved her words aside.

"Come—what was wrong with her? Was she buck-toothed, liver-spotted, what?"

"I do not know. I suppose she was passingly fair," he shrugged.

"You do not know?" the Marchioness repeated, drawing out each word. "What was the purpose of your visit, if not to inspect the girl?"

"I did. She did not suit my taste."

"What does taste have to do with marriage? You need an heir, not to be diverted by some woman 'of your taste.' What of your promise to me?" she demanded.

"The need for an heir has been impressed upon me," the Marquess answered with quiet bitterness, "and my word has always been kept. You will have your damnable heir, but I will not tie myself for life to such a henwitted, trembling chit as Buckley's daughter."

"Trembling, eh? Then you need to look among the more seasoned prospects. I know Lady Monroe has a widowed daughter who is still quite young enough to—"

"No!"

"More of Duard's ill-mannered ways? We will continue this conversation when you have overcome your rudeness," she snapped, struggling upright.

Rising, he reached to take her arm. Haughtily, she motioned him away. "I am not in my dotage as you would perhaps like to believe. Stay here and finish your brandy; it may soothe your temper," she dismissed him. "This will be concluded when we sup."

Once in the hall, the Marchioness ordered the footman to summon the Marquess's valet, Gideon, to her sitting room. As he went off, she raised her voice and called Jane.

The large, elderly woman came quickly, towering over the petite, aristocratic figure of her mistress. Wordlessly, she placed her arm about the Marchioness's waist and took her free hand, helping her up the grand staircase to her rooms.

"I shall rest upon the settee in my sitting room. My grandson's man will be here shortly."

Jane settled her mistress, fluffing pillows and covering her with a shawl. A knock sounded and she went to the door. Allowing Gideon to enter, the abigail clicked her tongue as she saw that Lady Longeton had risen to a sitting position and had pushed the shawl aside. With a slight, displeased curtsy, she withdrew.

Eyeing the Marchioness warily, Gideon bowed and awaited her demand.

"The Buckley chit—you saw her?" clipped the old woman bluntly. "How were her looks?"

"There are those who would find her fair—in a thin fashion," the valet answered carefully.

"She was not unduly unpleasant in appearance?"

"No, my lady."

"Was her manner displeasing—has she taken after her mother?"

"I . . . I," Gideon stammered, "I do not know the Baroness, my lady. I saw nothing objectionable about the young miss."

"Were you surprised by the sudden withdrawal of his lordship? Come, man, answer me! Do not stand there like a statue," the Marchioness snapped.

"To the truth, my lady, yes. It did appear that his lordship had taken to Miss Buckley; why he even allowed the miss's young brother to visit with him in his rooms."

"What did you overhear of their conversations?"

Drawing himself up proudly, Gideon stated, "I do not eavesdrop on my lord."

"Of course not," Lady Longeton soothed him, "but you must have unavoidably heard part of their words," she prodded while restraining her annoyance.

"Very little, my lady." Then, as he felt the Marchioness's sharp eyes steady upon him, he added, "I do believe something was said of a Thomas—no, Tommy, I believe the boy called—" He halted, evidently perplexed.

"What is bothering you now?"

"Now that I dwell on it a bit, my lady, I am certain the boy was speaking of his governess—a niece of the Buckleys. It seemed she had taken a fall while out riding and his lordship was somewhat concerned. Strangely enough, none of the servants ever spoke of the incident."

A smile appeared upon the Marchioness's face. "A fall, eh? Was there anything unusual about this governess?"

"I did not see her, my lady. The servants spoke well of her and appeared surprised to learn she was allowed to attend the soiree in honour of his lordship. It appears the girl is treated more as a"— he coughed delicately—"as a servant than as family."

"Do you know which branch of the family she is from?"

"The Baron's—his sister's only child, I gathered from the talk."

"The name?"

"Thait, I believe, my lady."

"Of the gentility, then," she mused to herself. Leaning back, she waved her hand. "You may go, Gideon. You need not mention this conversation to my grandson."

Bowing, Gideon departed with a breath of relief.

Thait, thought the Marchioness. I feel the name should mean something to me. Ah, well, when I am rested I shall think on it. Closing her eyes, she was instantly asleep.

Jane entered and re-covered her, shaking her head. This betrothal will be the end of her—or give her a reason to continue on, she swore.

Supper had been a silent affair. Longeton pushed his food about, eating little.

"I shall remain with his lordship while he takes his port," Lady Longeton told Eaken as the dishes were being removed. "Serve it and you may go. Close the doors behind you."

Settling back in his chair, the Marquess awaited he assault.

"Did you find the Baron well?" the Marchioness began conversationally.

He nodded.

"And his wife?"

A nod answered once again.

"I have been thinking that you were, perhaps, too hasty in your decision. The girl could be invited to spend a week at

Thornhill. You could come to know her better."

Longeton sipped his port. "No."

"Come now. Humour an old woman. What harm could be done? The entire family would be invited."

Cocking his head, the Marquess studied his grandmother. She was plotting, but what? "This is your home as well as mine. You may invite to it whomever you choose," he answered.

"But would you agree to entertain a summer party for me? We could invite some of your acquaintances, a nicely mixed group, a few choices from the marriage mart. . . ." She paused and changed tactics as a scowl appeared on her grandson's face. "Can I help it if some invited are of marriageable age and circumstances? It will be a simple group of young men and women, a few parents, and someone to amuse me—with simple entertainment."

Longeton hooted, "Gram, overdone—when did you ever have 'simple' entertainment at Thornhill?"

"Your appearance is much improved with a smile upon your features. It brings to mind your grandfather," she said sadly, then slapped the table. "It is settled then, I shall invite the Buckleys, including of course their niece, whom I understand has come to live with them." Pausing, she studied his features, which were now masked. With satisfaction, she rushed on. "You may, of course, submit the names of those you wish included. I will fill it out for an even number." She smiled approvingly at Longeton. "Yes, Thornhill should be much improved by the presence of young people, will it not?"

The Marquess did not answer, for his mind was taken with the thoughts of one certain young person and the possible consequences of her presence at Thornhill.

CHAPTER 11

Day by day the week of the summer party drew nearer. June turned to July as Lady Longeton watched her grandson bury himself ever deeper in the affairs and details of the estate. His days were spent closeted with his agents or in long hours riding, inspecting and visiting the farms and cottages of the estate; his nights were passed staring long hours into space or holding a book before him without turning more than a page.

All his actions increased the Marchioness's confidence in her decision and she greeted the morn of the Monday appointed for the arrival of the guests with an exuberance unfelt for many years.

It was late afternoon when Jane woke Lady Longeton from her nap.

"Has everyone arrived?" she asked as the abigail helped her dress.

"Yes, they are all accounted for."

"Did his lordship greet any of the guests personally?"

"I do not believe so. Eaken said he left following an early breakfast and was expected to return only shortly before supper is to be served."

"Good. I want to see his first reaction to the guests. Finish the buttoning—quickly! I wish to go down early."

As was her wish, Lady Longeton was the first to arrive in the main salon, where the guests would gather before going in to dine. Taking a seat that provided a good view of both the doors and the main portion of the room, she arranged her skirts skillfully. *They may say I am aged*, she thought, *but they find only the facade has changed. If I use my wits, this week will prove most profitable.*

The first to join the Marchioness were Lord

John Tuttle, a friend of Longeton's and his young sister, Lady Terese. Sir Peter Appleton, another schoolfriend of the Marquess's, greeted Lady Longeton with an exaggerated bow and solemnly kissed her hand.

"Still the flatterer, Peter," she laughed. "We should invite you more often. Nothing warms the heart of an old woman as quickly as a young rogue such as yourself."

"Old, my lady?" said Sir Peter. "Why, if you had but two score years less and I two score years more, we would make a match of it."

This remark elicited much laughter from those present, interrupted as Eaken announced the Buckleys.

Lady Longeton watched their entrance with great interest. She had known the present Baron's grandfather and judged him to be of the same ilk as he introduced his haughty, commoner wife. Lady Augusta gushed shrilly at the Marchioness—whose smile never wavered.

The Baroness drew a breath, giving Lady Longeton an opening. "This is your daughter, Baron?"

Proudly, he handed Dianna forward. The

young girl curtsied deeply and would not raise her eyes to meet the commanding face of the Marchioness.

"I trust you shall enjoy your visit here, child," Lady Longeton greeted her pleasantly.

"You were most gracious to invite us," Dianna answered, after an anxious glance at her mother.

Mentally tallying a point in favour of the Marquess's judgment as she inwardly quivered at this faint echo of Lady Augusta, Lady Longeton beckoned Thomasina forward.

"Why do you hang back, child?" she scolded lightly. "And this," she said to the Baron, "is Helena's daughter? I was saddened to hear of your poor sister's death."

"Yes, most tragic. But we have the joy of Thomasina's presence. Come forward," he beckoned. "You must forgive her," he said in an undertone, "she is shy in society."

Lady Longeton did not find the rebellious eyes, sparking their displeasure and which were not lowered as the girl sank into her curtsy, shy. The look was proud, daring fault to be found. The Marchioness bowed her head in answer to the curtsy, a glimmer of amusement coming over her features. "I believe you know Lord Tuttle, Baron. John, will you introduce everyone? My voice is not as strong as it once was."

The round of introductions was halted temporarily by the arrival of Lord and Lady Sherrad, Viscount Sherrad, and his brother, Nicholas. Entering with them was Lord Stone, a neighbor of the Marchioness and near her age, who it appeared, had brought an uninvited guest.

After the acknowledgments and introductions were completed, he seated himself on a chair beside the Marchioness. "I trust you shall not mind my having brought an extra—I know how you detest odd numbers at dinner." He motioned towards the dandy who had arrived with him. "George arrived just today for a visit. You recall Lord Sternbye—'Bent for Hell' Sternbye they called him," Lord Stone chuckled. "It appears the pit's fallen near the trunk with this one," he added in an undertone as he bent near Lady Longeton. "George has just returned from a tour of Italy."

The dandy spied his host seated with Lady

Longeton and swaggered forward. Reaching for Lady Longeton's hand, he dropped a wet kiss upon it. "Most kind of you to allow me to be present," he said oilily. "Lord Stone has spoken of you often and I find your beauty as true as he pictured it for me."

Lady Longeton dismissed him with a nod. "How long is he to be visiting?" she asked.

"I fear the entire week," sighed Lord Stone. "His father thought he could benefit from my years of maturity. I like not what I have heard of him nor what I have seen. It is rumoured he has nearly ruined the family with his excesses and scrapes. Do not fear, though. I have warned him to be on his best behaviour," he assured her with a pat to her hand.

"I shall not worry about it. I am certain Brutus will manage him quite well. It is only for a week; at least you shall be spared, for I am certain he will take it upon himself to invite himself to all our functions. Do not frown—there will be no harm done. It may even prove diverting. Ah, here are the Claymores and their two lovely young daughters."

Lady Claymore greeted the Marchioness

with a kiss on the cheek and presented her daughters, Ann and Mary.

"The girls have certainly grown," commented Lord Stone. "You must be proud to have two such lovely young ladies in your household."

"Yes, Lord Claymore and I are most pleased—and happy that the girls have been included in your plans. It is shameful that we do not visit more often—the distance is so brief." She glanced at the others in the room. "But I do not see Lord Brutus."

"He will be here shortly. Estate affairs have kept his hours filled of late," Lady Longeton responded.

Introductions were made once more and polite conversation ensued as the young people became acquainted and the men discussed politics, the women fashion. Lady Longeton kept one eye on the doorway, knowing her grandson disliked being announced.

Her watchfulness was rewarded as she saw him quietly observing the guests. His eyes went over all then rested on one for a long moment before he stepped forward and greeted his grandmother.

Lord John and Sir Peter heard his voice and greeted him boisterously.

Lady Longeton signaled Eaken to announce dinner while keeping her eyes on Thomasina.

The ladies had returned to the main salon, leaving the gentlemen to their port. Lady Augusta had kept a constant check upon Dianna during the meal and now took the opportunity of a lull in the older women's conversation to observe her once again.

The five young women were gathered about the piano. May and Ann Claymore were playing while all joined in the singing. Happening to catch her daughter's eye, Lady Augusta nodded approvingly and Dianna weakly smiled back.

She fits in, proper as any, the Baroness thought. There shall be no problem now. Thinking back to the day Longeton bolted from Buckley House, she wondered how they could have been so wrong. It was all so clear now; his lordship had simply panicked at the last moment, as men were certainly prone to do when it came to marriage. Dianna would not fail at this second chance. She had instructed her daughter long and well in what was expected of her. There would be no more missish behaviour about the Marquess being sinister—the girl took after her father. That had been dealt with this month past, she thought. Ah, yes, entirely, she thought with complete satisfaction.

Even her husband's joining the young women in song when the men returned to the salon did not disturb her overly much, although he did seem out of place with Sir Peter and Lord John.

Lady Claymore signaled an early end to the gay evening by announcing that they must depart, as the tour of the ruins was set for midmorn of the next day.

Objections were raised by the young men, but Lady Longeton, rising, silenced them. "Your sorrow shall be brief, my fine young gentlemen," she teased. "You have only a few short hours before you all will be gathered together to explore Haunt Haven."

The Claymore girls and Dianna giggled nervously. Lady Terese whispered to Thomasina, "It is said to be the haven of a group of quite wicked ghosts. Is it not wonderful?" she twittered.

Suppressing the desire to roll her eyes in disgust, Thomasina nodded noncommitally. Somehow she did not find the prospect of visiting ghosts—even vile ghosts—as disturbing as spending a week at Thornhill. The evening's gaiety had been clouded for her by the brooding presence of the Marquess, who had joined in only nominally, remaining for the largest part of the evening with the older gentlemen, despite his grandmother's displeased grimaces whenever he chanced to look in her direction.

Wraps were brought to ward off the evils of a damp summer chill and the bidding of good-byes began. Lady Longeton and her grandson were busily doing so when Dianna joined Thomasina with an unladylike poke.

"Isn't that Lord Sternbye handsome?"

Thomasina eyed the dandy's green and yellow striped frock coat and canary-yellow pantaloons. A quick glance at her cousin told her the girl was not joking. "He sets a different style," she whispered back charitably. Looking back to the admired figure she could not help contrasting it to Longeton's graceful form in the smooth-fitting gray cutaway and skin-hugging white breeches, which she had to admit showed his leg most favourably. Her eyes traveled up his form, admiring it against her will.

Lord Longeton turned his head as Lord Stone approached to bid farewell and his eyes locked with Thomasina's as he shook hands with the elderly man.

"Very pleasant evening, Brutus. How is Rapscallion? Brutus?" he repeated, becoming aware the Marquess's attention was not upon him. Turning, he saw it was Thomasina the man was looking at. Giving Longeton a nudge, he said, "Most interesting week you shall have." He chuckled good-naturedly.

"Good evening to you," Longeton said, ignoring Lord Stone's words. "Do come again soon, my lord."

"My pleasure, Brutus. Good eve to you, my lady." He bowed before the Marchioness with a knowing wink.

Casting a look back to Thomasina, Longeton's hopeful face became masked as he saw Viscount Sherrad whispering with her, far too intimately.

CHAPTER 12

The early light cast a pale shadow outside the window as Thomasina looked across the garden below. A glance at the bed assured her that Dianna was still asleep.

She gazed for a brief time at the sleeping form of her cousin, thinking of the change that had occurred in the girl over the last month. A new civility was apparent in all her relationships, especially with Parker, to whom she had come to show kindness. Even Thomasina was no longer subjected to her haughtiness and gibes. Dianna had made no objection when she learned they must share a room at Thornhill; such acceptance on her part would have been unthinkable a month past.

Shaking her head, she turned her eyes back to the window, wondering what Aunt Augusta would do if she knew her lengthy lectures were having an opposite effect.

These thoughts brought a yearning for physical activity as she found her mind leaping even closer to the Marquess. Quietly, she tiptoed from the room into the deserted hall. No one had yet risen, nor were they likely to, she thought, for some time. With vigorous steps she paced down the hall, pausing only when she came to an intersection. The second corridor had a bright red rug running down the center and the walls on either side were lined with full-length portraits. On the right were what appeared to be past Marquesses of Thornhill, judging from the resemblance to the present one she noted in their features. The formal attire placed them in their own time period, and they seemed to stare disapprovingly at her. To the left, the wives stared haughtily from their height, seemingly disliking the inspection of a stranger. Thomasina studied each portrait as she moved slowly down the corridor.

"Well, Lord Brutus, you come by your grimness naturally enough," she said to herself. "A more dour set of ancestors I have yet to see."

"Miss Thait, her ladyship desires to speak with you."

Whipping about, Thomasina's heart momentarily lurched as she took in Jane's towering bulk.

"This way, miss," the abigail ordered, stalking to a door and motioning Thomasina forward.

With the wish that she had remained in her room, Thomasina stepped gingerly into the sitting room. Jane followed upon her heels. "In the hall studying the portraits, my lady. A point for you," the abigail said in an odd sort of introduction that mystified Thomasina who watched the Marchioness nod knowingly.

"You are an early riser, Miss Thait—I like that," Lady Longeton said in greeting as Jane withdrew.

Involuntarily, Thomasina's head went up

proudly, her face a clear reflection of her thought that she did not need nor care for the Marchioness's approval.

"I understand you are one and twenty," Lady Longeton continued as she raised her quizzing glass and studied Thomasina's form quite deliberately from the copperish curls to the hem of her day gown.

Anger, not embarrassment, at this examination tinged the girl's cheeks as she strove to control the dislike she suddenly felt for the haughty, aristocratic lady before her.

"Be seated, Miss Thait," Lady Longeton said slowly, lowering her quizzing glass to her lap. The two women gazed at each other intently, the older judging the other's mettle, the younger recalling her mother's admonition of kindness to all elderly whatever their habits.

"Why do you take me in such distaste, Miss Thait?" Lady Longeton asked bluntly.

Thomasina gave a small gasp. "My lady, I meant no offense. Pardon me for being so bold," she said lowering her eyes.

"Young woman, at my age I do not have time to sort out riddles. Speak plainly, if you please," the Marchioness demanded.

"I . . . I meant I was sorry for staring at you so," Thomasina explained, raising her eyes.

Lady Longeton let out a hoot of laughter. "Is that what the young are taught? No wonder I can never get anyone to look directly at me," she said with a smile. "That is better," she continued as she saw Thomasina relax. "Now, take the chair as I bade you. I wish to learn more of your life."

Biting back a retort, Thomasina wondered at the old woman's callousness. Was not the fact that her grandson had caused the death of her parents enough knowledge?

"The Thait family is not very large, is it? I believe your father was a younger son," the Marchioness said. "I must apologize for knowing so little of your family. I have lost contact with many as I have grown older. The Baron told me you lost your parents little more than a year past—how tragic to lose both. I do not recall hearing of their deaths, but we lost my grandson near the same time."

"I am sorry," Thomasina said sincerely as she saw the Marchioness's pained expression.

"No, no. It is always best to go forward, as

I am certain you have learned. Do you enjoy living with the Buckleys?"

"My uncle is . . . kind."

"When his wife allows it, I should think," Lady Longeton rejoined.

Eyes widened at such outspokenness; Thomasina wondered what next she would hear. A grudging respect for the grande dame sprang up within her.

"Ah, you know not what to think of my tongue. That is as it should be, for no one seems to know what to make of it," she chuckled gleefully, then became serious. "Would you care to leave the Buckleys—perhaps for a household of your own?" she asked with deft swiftness.

A burst of laughter was free before Thomasina realized it. A shamefaced glance at the Marchioness found her to be, strangely enough, not insulted at the response but beaming with approval.

"Answer me, miss."

"In truth, my lady, I do desire to find a position as governess in some good household, but as to establishing one of my own, that is quite impossible. My father died impoverished." Thoughts raced through her mind. The Marchioness must have been kept unknowledgeable of her grandson's dissolute living, although Thomasina found it hard to believe this particular old woman would be unknowledgeable about anything.

"Is something the matter, child?" Lady Longeton asked, wondering at the strange expression that had come over the girl.

"No, my lady. I simply meant that I could not set up a household of my own, and dowerless, marriage is also out of the question."

"What if a lack of dowry did not have a bearing on a proposal of marriage?" the Marchioness asked, watching Thomasina carefully.

A grin appeared in answer to Lady Longeton's question. "My lady, my dowerless state has proven a powerful protection from marriage proposals, and I must admit I have found that to be a relief."

"Folderal. You cannot mean you do not desire to have a home and children—a husband is necessary for such accomplishments," admonished the Marchioness.

"Then I must forego the necessity as well as the reality," Thomasina said bluntly.

"You have no wish to marry—not even a wealthy man?"

"Not I," clipped Thomasina adamantly.

The wisdom of age detected the brief flicker of anguish that came with the terse answer. "You would not consider the proposal of a wealthy man?"

"If I must ever consider an offer for my hand, it will be the man's honour that I scrutinize more closely than his material wealth," Thomasina replied with an edge of bitterness to her voice.

"What an odd answer for one in your state," the Marchioness noted. "But I do believe you are sincere."

With a brief nod from the other, Thomasina found herself dismissed. "I am tired, Miss Thait. You should return to your room. Enjoy your excursion later this morn."

Rising, Thomasina bobbed a curtsy and withdrew, puzzled by the interview and its purpose. It was no more baffling than her invitation to Thornhill, and she did not care to dwell upon the objective of the latter. Picking up her skirts, she raced back to the room she shared with Dianna.

Her cousin sat up as she slipped quietly

into the room and closed the door. "Why have you been about so early, Thomasina?" she asked. A mournful expression came over her, and she raised her hand to her face and paled. "An assignation," she breathed, and fell upon her pillow in a burst of tears leaving Thomasina staring at her dumbfounded.

In Lady Longeton's rooms, Jane had returned.

"Well, Jane?"

"Cocky, my lady."

"Exactly. Yes, I believe she will do very well, but I feel there is some impediment. It may take some doing." Thumping the cup and saucer upon the table spilling the cocoa, she ordered, "Dress me, Jane. I must see that grandson of mine."

CHAPTER 13

A soft sigh came from Thomasina as she noted with relief that Dianna was responding quite happily to Lord Sternbye's words as they rode together, the morning's outburst forgotten. A glance to her left at Mathew revealed that he had noticed Dianna's enjoyment of Lord George's attention also.

"Why must we be last?" Parker asked unhappily from her right.

"You should be grateful for being allowed to join us, instead of spending the day with your mother," Viscount Sherrad admonished him. "Only Tommi's willingness to have you is responsible for your coming."

"It does not matter where we are placed in the ride," Thomasina added. "All are enjoying the same fair day."

"But I wished to see Haunted Haven first," Parker grumbled.

"You may not see it first," Thomasina laughed, "but I have no doubt you will explore more of it than all the others."

"Someone is coming," Parker shouted as he spied a lone rider topping the knoll of a rise to one side.

As everyone cast about for a glimpse, Lord John pointed and said, "That is Brutus. Lady Longeton said he would join our party. Let us halt and allow him to overtake us."

Horses were reined to a stop and all watched the galloping steed.

"That is Rapscallion," Parker said excitedly. "Look at how he runs!"

"I told you he was swift," Nicholas Sherrad said as he watched the steed's movements appreciatively.

The Marquess's stallion thudded to a halt before the group, causing the other mounts to shift nervously. Dianna gave a shriek and jerked on the reins as her steed stepped back.

Lord Sternbye grabbed the bridle and made a huge show of settling the animal. "Are you quite all right, my dear Miss Buckley?" he gushed. "How ungentlemanly of the Marquess," he added to her in an undertone that carried through the group.

With a grateful nod, she assured him, "I am quite fine now, thank you, Lord Sternbye. I do not know what I would have done had you not been so quick."

"My honoured privilege," he replied with a flourish. "For one as beautiful as you, there is little I would not do."

The Claymore girls and Lady Terese twittered at hearing this exchange, while eyebrows rose among the gentlemen who could see little danger in a mount's shifting back a few steps. Only Lord Longeton took outward displeasure at the words.

Misinterpreting the reason for his reaction, Thomasina urged her steed forward, calling Parker to join her. To her great annoyance, the boy called out to the Marquess, "Your lordship, will you not ride with us?"

Longeton's frown lessened as his eyes met

the boy's. He glanced at Thomasina, and she looked away deliberately. Seeing that Lord John had joined Sternbye and Dianna, he set his jaw and reined Rapscallion beside the boy's pony. "You know our direction," he called to Sir Peter. "Lead on."

Slowly the group wended forward, conversation breaking out among the various riders.

"That's a top o' the trees beast," Parker said, imitating conversation he had overheard as he eyed Rapscallion enviously.

"Someday I may let you ride him," Longeton told him. "But he would prove too much for you at this time. I hope you have found Blackie satisfactory."

"At least he is faster than Toby," Parker acknowledged.

"Miss Thait, I hope you have recovered completely from your fall," the Marquess said, looking past Parker at Thomasina.

"There was nothing to recover from, your lordship," she answered tonelessly, refusing to look at him. "I am relieved to see that Rapscallion has suffered no lasting effects from his injury."

Hoping that Tommi would be diverted by

the Marquess, Parker urged Blackie to a faster pace, pulling ahead of the pair.

"Parker!" Thomasina called.

"Let the boy go ahead," Longeton enjoined her as he drew Rapscallion nearer her mount. "We can see him and I can catch him easily if you feel it necessary." He smiled at the look of total annoyance she threw at him.

"Don't you feel you are neglecting your guests, your lordship?" Thomasina asked irritably.

"They appear well satisfied at the moment, and as they are not my guests I shall not be unduly troubled about their comforts."

"But—"

"They are my grandmother's guests. The duties I fulfill as host are to humor her only," he ended dryly.

"Do not overextend yourself on my behalf, 'Lord Br—your lordship," Thomasina tossed out, catching herself just in time. Irked at her near slip, she tapped her mount with the riding crop, causing it to break into a canter. Longeton loosened Rapscallion's reins and the stallion kept pace easily.

They passed Lord John and Dianna, whom

Parker had joined, and the boy called out, "A race. Let us race!"

The gentlemen, eager for a faster pace, joined in as did the ladies except for Dianna. Lord George slowed his mount when he saw that she was not joining the gallop and paced his mount with hers.

"One would think they are in their salad days," he quipped, motioning to those leaving them behind. "How very pleasant to have someone who enjoys a leisurely ride such as I do, in my company."

Diana blushed at the flattery, while enjoying it immensely.

"We shall arrive last, Miss Buckley, but who is to say our journey shall not be the more delightful?" Lord George said with a meaningful tap to his lightly powdered cheek.

A wavering smile answered his words. *How pleasant he is,* thought Dianna. *Not constantly frowning and scowling. A true gentlemen in word and deed; if only the Marquess were so attentive it would be far easier to bear the thought of marriage.* Biting her lip at the thought, she looked ahead at the galloping riders. Viscount Sherrad was nearing Longeton, who was leading.

Oh, Mathew, she thought despairingly.

"Miss Buckley, have I offended you?" Lord George implored with false sincerity.

"Of course not, my lord," Dianna answered, her attention diverted from the other riders. "You are most . . . amiable."

With a knowledgeable, smirking smile, Lord George acknowledged the compliment and settled back in his saddle, thoroughly satisfied with his progress.

After the excitement of the gallop and the exertion of the ride, the young ladies insisted upon resting and partaking of the cold luncheon that the Marchioness had sent ahead to the ruins with Lady Augusta and Lady Claymore. The footmen had arranged the tables for them in the shade of the trees on the east side of the ruins.

Thomasina was grateful for the help of Mathew and Nicholas in keeping Parker restrained from dashing among the ruins on his own.

The ladies restored and appetites satisfied, the party was ready to ramble through the ruins of the ancient hill fort. Taking Parker's hand firmly in her own, Thomasina listened as Lady Claymore admonished everyone to stay together. The members of the exploring band were careful to follow the warning until out of the older ladies' sight. As they walked further on, the band slowly separated as one pair then another trio voiced interests in different areas of the ruins.

Viscount Sherrad bent to whisper to Thomasina, and Parker took advantage of the momentary distraction to break free of her grip and scamper over the earthenwork mound ahead of them.

"Drat!" Thomasina swore as she watched him quickly disappear from sight.

"I may catch him if I go around the earthenworks," Mathew told her. "You see to it he doesn't come back this way."

Striding to the edge of the earthenworks as the Viscount ran to go around it, Thomasina caught sight of Parker scrambling through the rubble near one of the outer buildings.

He will be long gone by the time Mathew reaches that side, she thought. *I had best try to follow and keep him within sight.*

Rushing along the steep edge looking for a

place to descend, Thomasina slipped and slid down the fifteen-foot embankment, landing with a jarring thump. On her feet instantly, she ran forward, contemplating the retribution she would extract from Parker for this escapade.

Parker saw her approach and charged off in the direction of a crumbling tower.

"Parker, come back this instant!" she shouted. "Mathew, the tower," she cried over her shoulder, hoping he was near enough to hear her.

The tower had once stood over forty feet tall but had slowly disintegrated, so now only twenty feet remained. Stones of all sizes littered the ground inside and out; and the only remaining feature within it was a stone stairway that wound around the inner wall. Parker was well over halfway up the stairs when Thomasina reached the tower's entrance.

Her usual common sense had been so thoroughly ruffled by the slide down the earthenworks and the awkward running over the stony ground in riding boots that, without a thought to the consequences, she hiked her skirts up a bit higher and took the crumbling steps two at a time, intent upon capturing the boy.

Seeing Thomasina so near, Parker turned and halted. The stairs had only a width of eighteen inches, but seeing the glint in Thomasina's eyes, he decided to try and dodge past her.

"Tommi!"

The shout of her name drew both Thomasina's and Parker's eyes to the floor below. Longeton stood in the center glaring up at them in concern.

Parker's eyes swung from him to Thomasina and back. Bolting down the steps past Thomasina, he knocked her off balance as she made a grab for him. For a moment she wavered as she fought to regain her equilibrium but lost it completely as a loose stone slipped from beneath her foot, sending her in a tumble of billowing petticoats towards the rock-strewn floor.

Terrified, Parker did not stop running when he realized Tommi was falling. Spurred by fear, he burst from the tower ruins, nearly leveling Mathew, who turned and gave chase.

Within the tower, Thomasina plummeted into the Marquess's outstretched arms, causing him to be seated in a rather perfunctory manner upon the rocky floor.

Dust settled in small swirls about them as they sat staring at each other, fear, concern, and astonishment mingled in their expressions. Parker, her parents' deaths, his pride and restraint; each was mindless of all but the person now so near.

Slowly Longeton reached out and touched Thomasina's cheek. "You are unharmed?" he asked in wonder.

"And you?" she asked.

A force neither could control drew their lips together in a soft lingering kiss. The mystery of love continued to hold them in its tender web as he drew her to him in a gentle embrace. Closing her eyes, Thomasina laid her head upon his shoulder, willing her mind free.

The fragile bond between the two was disturbed as she felt the Marquess suddenly squirm. Leaning back in his arms, she opened her eyes and encountered a broad grin upon Longeton's usually sombre features.

"When I admonished you not to be a 'green apple,'" he laughed softly, "I did not think you would next fall like an overripe pear! I must beg you rise, Tommi—for we have not chosen a bed of goosedown to rest upon." He drew a sharp-edged stone from beneath his thigh as proof.

Voices from without shattered the remaining magic and Thomasina scrambled to her feet.

Pushing Parker before him, Viscount Sherrad entered hurriedly. "Tommi, you are unhurt!" he exclaimed. "Parker said you had fallen from the stairs." His eyes shifted to the rising Marquess. "I have you to thank then, Lord Longeton," Mathew said, releasing Parker and grasping the Marquess's arm to assist him.

Inner turmoil stayed Thomasina from looking at Longeton, who was beseeching her to, with his eyes. She stepped towards Mathew.

"Thank God; Longeton was here," he said to her. "Are you certain no harm has come to you?"

Mutely, Thomasina nodded.

Holding her arm, the Viscount turned back to Longeton. "I thank you once again, my lord, for keeping Tommi from harm."

The plea on Longeton's face gradually hardened into an emotionless mask as he gave his own meaning to Sherrad's concern and Thomasina's refusal to look at him. His hat was snatched from the stone-littered floor and he strode through the entryway before further words could be spoken.

Thomasina, whom everyone knew never cried, looked up at Mathew, large tears brimming in her lashes.

"Why would you not speak to him? Has he played falsely with your affections?" Mathew asked her gently.

A shake of her head and a small sob came in answer.

Filled with compassion, he put his arms about her, trying to give comfort. "What has happened, Tommi?"

Raindrop tears followed one another slowly down her cheeks as she looked up. "It is ghastly," she choked, "for I think I love him." A bitter sob wrenched itself free and the Viscount held her close, patting her upon the back consolingly.

"Who is crying in there?" a high-pitched voice asked from without.

Mathew stiffened; he recognized the voice but it was too late to act.

A gasp escaped from Dianna when she saw

the two, Mathew's arms still about Thomasina. "Why . . . why . . ." she sputtered.

Lord George stuck his head around her to see what was about.

"Miss Thait took a nasty fall from the stairs and is quite shaken," Sherrad explained icily as Thomasina stepped away from him. "Master Parker was the cause of it."

The scrunch of stone against stone revealed the boy's presence as he shifted nervously.

"Yes, yes," Lord George said in a hollow imitation of belief. "Are you quite all right, Miss Thait?" he asked perfunctorily, making certain Dianna had time to take in the red-flamed embarrassment upon Thomasina's face.

"Dianna, you could help Tommi," Sherrad said pointedly.

"I beg you not to be so familiar, Lord Sherrad," Lord George admonished him. "You appear quite capable of . . . helping Miss Thait. Miss Buckley, my arm."

Placing her hand upon Sternbye's proffered arm, Dianna cast a look of contemptuous anger at Thomasina and Mathew before allowing him to lead her from the tower.

His features, angry and dismayed in turn, changed visibly as Sherrad watched the two depart.

"I am so sorry, Mathew. I have ruined it all for you," Thomasina said on the verge of tears once more, a strain of bitterness and hopelessness creeping into her voice.

"No, all is not lost—you shall see," he said comfortingly as he took her hand. "A skirmish lost does not lose the battle."

"The battle was lost ere it began," she answered.

He looked at her, searching for the meaning of her words.

Giving his hand a squeeze, she tried to smile. "I shall speak to Dianna—to explain this."

Mathew continued to stare at her; then he glanced at the figures of the retreating pair. "Perhaps you are correct, Tommi," he said slowly. "There can be no victory if the battle is lost before it is begun. "Mayhaps," he continued, turning to her and taking her other hand, "we should both look no further than our agreement."

CHAPTER 14

"Her ladyship desires to speak with you, my lord," Gideon informed the Marquess. "She said she will await you in your sitting room."

Longeton nodded as he shrugged into a fresh coat. A quick washing and fresh garments had lightened his mood somewhat, but he was in no frame of mind for a scolding from his grandmother for returning to Thornhill long before the others did.

"I was disappointed in not being able to speak with you before you departed this morn," the Marchioness said as he stepped into the sitting room.

"There were matters that needed attention."

"There is only *one* matter that I care to have you attend to at this time," she reproved him gently.

His brooding eyes narrowed.

"I wish to speak to you about Miss Thait," she went on pointedly.

"Gram, it does not concern you. Leave it lie," Longeton snapped angrily.

Hobbling painfully, Lady Longeton went to the sofa. Once seated, she patted the cushion beside her.

With a tired shake of his head and a sad shrug of his shoulders, the Marquess joined her.

Her small, aged hand touched his strong, clenched fist. "You have raised your voice seldom to me," she mused. "Do you recall the first time you did so?"

He shook his head numbly.

"It was many years ago. Your father was planning to sell a colt you had raised. I was speaking to you of something one day at this time—about what, I disremember—when you snapped at me, then burst into tears. Your sharp words then were caused by the ache of a breaking heart." She nodded sadly as she looked upon his troubled features. "You are too much a man to cry now, but I feel—sense—that the cause of your curtness is the same as long ago."

Longeton turned from her gaze, his body rigid.

"Those many years ago I healed the wound; I bought the colt and gave him back to you. Can you not trust me once more to aid you?"

"Not all problems can be solved by wealth," he said tersely, rising.

"No, but a loving heart can give consolation when there is nothing to be done. It is the Thait chit that troubles you, is it not?"

"Thomasina is no mere chit," he retorted, his anger flaring again. "She. . . ." He fell silent.

" . . . is a very fortunate young woman to have my grandson love her." The Marchioness completed his sentence, forcing back a sudden swell of tears. "Have you quarreled with her?"

"We have not even truly spoken to one another," he said, taking his seat beside his grandmother once more. "Our relationship appears destined to be of a 'physical' nature."

Lady Longeton arched her brow. "Upon my soul!"

A ghost of a smile came to Longeton. Briefly he recounted the fall Thomasina had taken from Grandee and the incident in the tower ruins, editing both scenes as he saw fit.

"There are far more pleasant ways to become acquainted," she noted with mock seriousness.

Rising abruptly, the Marquess paced a few steps and turned. "There are moments when I am certain of her affection, but whenever we speak, she puts up a barrier—as if some reason existed for bitterness and hatred towards me."

"Have you questioned her about this?"

"Questioned? Spoken? Ha! We have exchanged far more bruises than words," he said heatedly.

Suppressing a smile, she asked, "Could it be pride that causes the barrier? Did you know that she is dowerless?"

"I did not and I care not," he retorted. "Thornhill never suffered unduly from

Duard's excesses. Fortunately he won more often than he lost. The neglect of the estate has been cared for. I have no need of a dowry."

"But it could be very important in her mind. Miss Thait may feel it humiliating to come to a marriage penniless," Lady Longeton reasoned. His doubtful look brought a second thought to mind. "Or do you fear she cares for another?" she asked bluntly. "And do not say you do not wish to speak of it," she cautioned him as he gave her a black look, "for if you do not speak with me, I shall speak with Miss Thait."

"You are utterly unprincipled, Gram. Underhanded—"

"Your grandfather appreciated my qualities, also," she interrupted him. "More to the point—you believe she cares for young Viscount Sherrad."

Cocking his head, Longeton viewed his grandmother with new discernment, a renewed respect.

"There is only a fraternal attachment there," the Marchioness sought to assure him. "I have observed them together. Each cares for the other, but it is only in friendship."

Longeton considered her words, points for and against her judgment ranging through his thoughts.

"You concede I am correct," Lady Longeton stated matter-of-factly. "There are but two choices before you."

Amused interest played across Longeton's features as he awaited her announcement of what she perceived his options to be.

"You can put the Thait chit from your mind and offer for the Buckley chit. Taken from her mother's influence I have no doubts she could be molded rather well." Pausing, she studied his reaction, then continued, "or you can offer for Miss Thait. Once you are betrothed, there will be ample time and opportunity to settle whatever misunderstandings have developed." The Marchioness fell silent as a thought nudged against her consciousness. "There is something about the name Thait that has been plaguing me. I wish you had not been out of the country before your brother's death—perhaps you could recall what. . . . No matter, it will come to me," she ended.

Longeton rose and paced to and fro, deep in thought. When he halted, he turned to his grandmother, held out his hand and helped her rise. "I will do as you suggest and approach Lord Buckley this very afternoon."

"But which shall you offer for?"

"That, you will learn this eve. Now, off to your rooms. You must rest for the evening's activities," he teased.

Managing a glare, Lady Longeton tossed her head proudly and slowly thumped from the room.

Jane opened the door for her as she approached her own sitting room. "A point for each of us," the Marchioness chuckled as she hobbled past the abigail into the room. "You were correct; he will make an offer this day and as I am certain of my point, see to the removal of all the glass and ceramic figurines, vases, et cetera, from the Baroness's rooms.

"Now you may help me to bed, for I may rest. We shall be closer to an heir by this eve," she ended, with complete, if not reliable, confidence.

CHAPTER 15

"Hur . . . rumph." The Baron loudly cleared his throat as he approached the tall figure staring out of the private study's windows. When there was no response, he asked, "Might I have a spot of brandy, my lord? A bit early, perhaps, but I feel the need of a drop or two."

"Of course," Longeton answered, and walked to the decanter. Pouring two generous glassfuls, he handed one to Buckley.

"To you and your good fortune," the Baron said, raising his glass in salute.

Both men took a healthy drink. The Marquess stepped back to his desk. "Please be seated, Baron," he said, sitting.

Doing as he was bid, the Baron leaned back comfortably and watched Longeton expectantly, thinking how pleased his wife would be with the news he would have for her when she returned from the outing.

"There is a matter of import I wish to discuss with you," Longeton began slowly.

Nodding happily, Buckley awaited further words as Longeton paused.

The beaming face before him was the cause of the Marquess's hesitation. It was a reminder of what the Baron expected, not unjustly, to hear. "First let me apologize. I fear a mistaken impression was given, which I must take responsibility for," he started again. Rushing on as a question replaced pleasure on the Baron's features, he explained. "The letter I wrote you mentioned the fact that I was seeking a bride and naturally you presumed that what I wrote pertained to your daughter. I hope there will be no undue upset feelings because of this mistaken impression.

"You see, Baron Buckley"— he paused but the Baron was no help —"I am approaching you for the hand of your niece Thomasina, in marriage."

For an instant the Baron sat as if he had not heard the Marquess's words. Then he said, "Thomasina? Marriage, eh? Good show, my boy. I congratulate you." Rising, he set his brandy on the desk separating them and reached across it for Longeton's hand.

"Then your consent is given?"

"Consent? Oh, not mine to give, you know. Tommi's of age. You will have to speak to her yourself," Buckley explained, pumping the Marquess's hand. "I could not be happier for you both."

"I hope Lady Augusta will share your feelings," Longeton said, disengaging his hand at last.

"Oh, dear me. 'Pon my soul," the Baron breathed, dragging a kerchief from his pocket as he settled heavily into his chair, mopping his forehead. "I suppose she must be told. Fine woman, my wife, you know—wouldn't have you think otherwise, but rather . . . rather excitable at times. Oh, my."

"May I suggest then, that you tell her nothing. Some women take, ah, 'disappointment,' shall we say, better in a group. Discourages hysterics, wouldn't you say?" Longeton offered.

"Hysterics. Oh, my." Buckley continued mopping his face. "You may have a point, my lord."

"Brutus, will do, Baron—after all, you are to be my uncle. I will make a point of thanking your dear wife this eve when the betrothal is announced," he added.

"Good show. Excellent idea. You are right. Best not to tell her anything. I shall say we discussed an enclosure bill if she learns of this meeting." Tucking his kerchief away in relief, the Baron raised his portly figure from the chair. "Congratulations, er, Brutus. I shall send Thomasina at once, er, well, as soon as I can speak to her privately." A huge gulp finished the brandy and he returned the glass to the desk. With a final handshake, he set out on his errand.

A few answers from Eaken told him Thomasina and Viscount Sherrad had returned from the outing alone, soon after the Marquess had, and that his niece had retired to her room. First he puzzled over why the three had returned without the others, then dismissed that as another idea came to him.

He demanded pen and paper. The note was completed and sealed in just a few moments. Handing it to Eaken, he ordered it delivered to Thomasina at once.

The maid bobbed a neat curtsy as Thomasina opened her door, then handed her the note. A quick glance took in the brief words. "There is no answer," Thomasina told the maid. "If you will tell me how to reach his lordship's study, I will go to my uncle as soon as I complete my toilet."

Thomasina paused before the study door, making certain of her composure. No idea of what her uncle could wish to speak to her about had presented itself. Lady Augusta could not have returned from the excursion to report what Dianna had surely imparted, so it could not be for that. Besides, if her aunt had returned, she reasoned, it would be she I would be seeing now. Reaching out, she opened the door and stepped in.

Please close the door," the Marquess requested as she halted just inside the study.

After complying, Thomasina glanced about for her uncle. "I understood my uncle wished to speak to me," she said when she realized he was not there.

"Did you not see him?"

"A note was brought to me requesting I speak with him here," she answered, puzzlement overtaking her quavering.

"The Baron is quicker-witted than his impression. It is I who desired to speak with you, Thomasina," he said, stepping around the desk to join her.

Backing from him, Thomasina said quietly, "There is nothing we can have to say to one another."

"I said *I* had something to say—to ask." With a frown he puzzled, "Why do you hold me in such dislike? I cannot believe you do."

Thomasina stood mutely rigid.

With a shake of his head, he turned and walked slowly to the window. As he stood facing it, he said, "I . . . I hold you in affection, Miss Thait, and it would please me if you would consent to be my wife." Longeton faced her. "Let me assure you there will be no difficulty about a dowry or its lack, and I am planning to make a generous settlement for you upon our marriage."

Astonishment held Thomasina speechless

until intense anger melted its shackles. "You are utterly contemptible," she breathed. "You *dare* to speak to me of marriage? What kind of man are you? Knowing you are the cause of my penniless state, you assure me of a 'generous settlement'? Is this how your conscience prompts you to act? Well, I will not assuage your guilt."

"I plan to announce our betrothal this eve when we sup," he said with cold persistence.

"I shall never agree to marry you."

"What choice do you have in the matter?" he asked, the ring of steel in his voice. "The Baroness will order you from Buckley when she learns of your refusal of my offer. What family will offer you a position when the matter is known?"

Truth echoed in his words. Thomasina ferreted wildly in her mind for an escape. Time, it told her, you must have time.

"I will announce our betrothal this eve, then?"

"There will . . . will be no denial."

"You consent?"

"No."

"You shall," Longeton replied stonily and turned back to the window.

Thomasina fled to the hall and raced for her room.

Staring unseeing at the scene before him, Longeton's mind seethed. "Why did I persist?" he asked himself. "What have I done? Lost all chance of. . . ."

An overview of all his actions with Thomasina brought to mind his brother's behaviour. *Am I no better than Duard?* he asked himself fearfully.

A long while later his mind suddenly recalled Thomasina's words: "knowing you caused my penniless state." What could she have meant? It made no sense; none of her accusations did.

Thait, he pondered. *No, I am certain I know nothing of the family.*

Gram. She will know what could have occurred between the families in the past.

Tension flowed from him as he strode hurriedly through the corridors to his grandmother's rooms, finding an outlet in the physical action and in the infinitesimal hope that he prayed his grandmother could keep safe.

CHAPTER 16

From end to end, across the room and back, Thomasina stalked agitatedly, her skirts swishing and swirling about her ankles. The whirlwind in her mind demanded some outlet and found it in this feverish movement. Faster and faster she moved until catching sight of her disquieted countenance in the looking glass above the dressing table, she halted, barely recognizing herself in this state.

Thomasina turned from the glass's accusation and stepped slowly to the open window. Gazing out onto the vast park before

Thornhill, she drew in deep breaths, slowly exhaling.

This frenzy will never do, ran through her mind. *You must concentrate.*

Somewhat calmer now, she found she *could* direct her thoughts to the Marquess, but that she did not *want* to.

This is ridiculous, she told herself, plopping upon the bed after her fourth false start in considering her dilemma. Instead of it, lace and silks had come to mind.

Why do I now think of shawls and gowns when I have never in the past? Her lower lip quivered and tears brimmed in her eyes as she admitted the answer. The thought of marriage to the Marquess was appalling because she loved him.

If I hated him, she thought, *I could endure marriage, but loving him, how am I to do it? Love can only be nurtured by the care of mutual respect and honour. How can I respect and honour a man who could take everything from a weak man such as my father? And worse, how can I endure a love which shall surely turn to hate?*

Thomasina looked about her room. It was not lavishly luxurious but so far above even the best room of the cottage she had shared with her mother that it made the comparison laughable. Would it be possible, she asked herself, for her to live here and not feel that she had betrayed her mother?

But it was not Longeton alone who gambled with your father—who lead him down the road of ruin, another corner of her mind told her. He did not force your father to hazard all—that was his own decision.

"I know," she cried aloud, "but why did it have to be he at all?" Rising in her turbulence, she returned to the window. *Oh, mother,* she thought, *am I also to marry a man whom I cannot hold in highest regard? At least you were spared the knowledge until you had shared some happiness.*

Do not marry him, then, her mind challenged her. The thought was considered—would she be strong enough to resist? *All he says is true—there would be none to turn to.*

What shall I do?

Thomasina had not been paying attention to what lay out the window, but now a group of riders followed by a carriage clattered into view.

Dianna! Lady Augusta! What was she to

tell them? A new storm gathered as she hopelessly watched them draw nearer and nearer.

Shall I skulk here like some guilty trollop? she pondered, anger rising within. No. Her aunt would be faced immediately. Besides, she thought, the public humiliation Aunt Augusta was capable of handing out to her should discourage the Marquess from his intent.

Assuring herself that she was completely composed, Thomasina tilted her head proudly and marched from the room, through the corridor. Her steps slackened as she descended the grand staircase. Once past midpoint she would be seen by all who entered.

One by one, she moved down the last dozen steps, watching the footmen open the doors and Eaken step out to welcome the returning guests.

Lady Terese and Nicholas Sherrad were the first to enter.

"Tommi," Nicholas shouted with relief, stepping towards her hurriedly. "You have recovered already?"

"What a pleasant surprise to find you here,"

said Lady Terese following Nicholas. "We did not know what to expect. Parker's story was so confusing."

Raising a hand to her mouth to stifle a gasp, Thomasina could only stare at them. How could she have forgotten Parker? Mathew had told the boy something after Dianna's departure from the tower, but what? Aunt Augusta would be more than furious at having him left on her hands.

"Miss Thait, are you quite uninjured?" Lord John asked, joining the group. "You do look quite pale."

"Oh, Thomasina, we are so relieved to see you," echoed the Misses Claymore.

Everyone surrounded her, speaking at once, peppering her with questions as to what had happened. Silence fell only when Lady Augusta piped a cough as she approached the group. Those about Thomasina fell back.

The Baroness, Parker in hand, halted before her niece, displeasure written in her every line. "Parker has imparted his part in the incident in the tower ruins," Lady Augusta began shrilly, "and I am most happy to find you unharmed by the fall you incurred because of my son. As his punishment he is to remain in his room until you give permission for him to leave it." Words apparently finished, she nodded curtly and sailed away. Parker, in tow, managed to throw a smile over his shoulder before they disappeared from sight.

Watching the last of Lady Augusta's billowing skirts as they skimmed across the floor in her wake, Thomasina could not believe her ears. Cautioned by her mind's words, her eyes scoured the small group for Dianna. Eaken's voice, raised in greeting, drew her glance to the doorway.

Lord George was bowing Dianna inside with an exaggerated flourish. Her eyes met Thomasina's, wavered, then turned away as she lifted her head haughtily and took Lord Sternbye's arm. With a smirking nod and a lift of his eyebrows, he acknowledged Thomasina's gaze.

Her dislike of Lord George took a huge leap at this gesture, and she felt a sudden fear for her cousin. Dianna would have to be warned to be wary of Sternbye, Thomasina sensed, but knew not how to impart it.

The thought was lost as the party began speaking about what to do. General agreement was reached by the group to retire to their rooms and freshen, with arrangements to meet in the gardens in the early evening before they dined.

Thomasina's steps back to her shared room were much slower than those that had lead her from it. Dianna had excused herself instead of visiting with everyone for those few minutes, and now awaited her. With chin uplifted, ready for the assault, Thomasina stepped into the room.

It was not the role of combatant, nor even of defendant, that awaited her, but that of consoler, for Dianna lay sprawled upon the bed, weeping with an intensity that tore at Thomasina's heart. There was naught she could do but wait for the worst of the storm to pass.

"Please, take this," Thomasina urged, holding out the dampened towel. "It will make your headache better."

Dianna reached for the towel sulkily but raised it eagerly to her red-blotched, swollen face.

"Will you not tell me what has upset you so?" Thomasina attempted once more. "Let me explain what happened in the tower." She lowered her head, a slight blush upon her cheeks. "I am most grateful you did not tell what you saw—it could be so easily misunderstood."

"You can thank Lord Sternbye," Dianna sniffled, "that I said nothing. He insisted there would be an end to all activities and that mother would drag us all home if she learned of your scandalous behaviour."

"There was nothing scandalous about my behaviour," Thomasina said, striving to control her temper. "Here, give me that towel and I will freshen it for you. We must do something about your face for there is only a short time before we are to rejoin the others." Thomasina rinsed and wrung the towel deftly. "What you saw in the tower," she began as she handed the towel back to her cousin, "was simply Mathew trying to console me as a brother would. There was nothing more in his actions."

"I cannot believe that," Dianna snuffled in reply. "Mathew has been overly attentive to you for some time. You replaced me in his affections long ago. Oh, what does it matter?

Mother insists I marry the Marquess." Tears welled brightly once more.

"Do not cry, Dianna. It will only make matters worse. You will only bring the swelling back. What will your mother say when she sees you if you continue to carry on so?"

The tears were frightened away by these words. Rising, Dianna went to the stand and washed her face. Patting it dry, she surveyed the damage. "Do you think the redness will depart in time?"

"If you remain calm, I am certain it will," Thomasina reassured her.

"Oh, Tommi—may I call you that?" A weak smile appeared as Thomasina nodded. "I must talk to someone or I shall simply die. Do you promise you will tell no one what I say?"

A knock on their door startled both girls. Lady Augusta steamed into the room, a reproving stare given to each. "So, you both have guilty consciences," she stated stridently, slamming the door closed behind her. "Now young misses, both of you, be seated," she commanded, pointing to the bed.

Sitting side by side, the girls were united by mutual dread.

"Thomasina, I do not care for you to be deceived by my words before the others. The incident in the tower was completely your responsibility due to your not controlling Parker. You shall henceforth be relieved of supervising him and shall do whatever errands and tasks Dianna and I find for you. When we return to Buckley House a suitable position shall be found for you.

"May I remind both of you young ladies that it is never proper to be alone with a gentleman for any reason. Let us hope tongues do not wag overly much about either of you," she staccattoed to a finish.

"Yes," both girls managed, eyes properly lowered.

"And you, miss," the Baroness said, turning the attack to her daughter, "you do not need to be reminded of our purpose here. It will not be accomplished if you continue to simper over that popinjay. I will not tolerate such behaviour."

"But—mama—"

"You dare to interrupt me," shouted Lady Augusta, and her hand dashed a slap across Dianna's face.

The young girl blanched and the Baroness paused as if regretting her action, but her determination drove her on. "I will have you betrothed to the Marquess. No one will snicker at me again behind my back when you are the Marchioness of Thornhill. It will be done—do you understand?"

Visibly shaken, Dianna nodded.

"Compose yourself—what have you been sniveling over this time? Never mind—make yourself fit to be seen and come to the gardens. You are to make yourself pleasant to his lordship." Abruptly Lady Augusta bent and kissed her daughter's cheek. "It is for your good I do this," she said in a milder tone. "I shall be watching your behaviour also," she warned Thomasina as long strides took her to the door. With one last warning look at both girls, she departed.

As the echo of Lady Augusta's steps faded, Thomasina laid her hand gently upon Dianna's. "I am sorry," she began.

"Do not," her cousin said, flinging the hand aside. "I do not need sympathy from you. How can you understand? My own mother condemns me to life with a glowering beast and you have Mathew's love." She bounded up from the bed. "How stupid I was to tease Mathew. If I had not, he might have offered for me before the Marquess wrote that horrid letter. Only Lord George understands. He is kind and considerate and—"

"You mustn't pay attention to what he says, Dianna," Thomasina cautioned her.

"And why not?" she demanded.

"I do not know—there is something false about him. We know nothing of his family or of him."

"He is of the gentry and mother would say that is all that matters, if it were not for the Marquess," Dianna retorted. "You are jealous because he has not flattered you," she finished cattily. "We had best go to the gardens or mother will scold us again."

"Dianna—"

"I will not listen. Are you coming with me?"

With a hopeless shrug at the ever growing waves swelling about her, Thomasina followed her cousin from the room with dragging steps.

CHAPTER 17

Tapping his powdered cheek, Lord George stood deep in concentration. The Buckley chit, while favouring him with smiles, was being kept from his side by her mother. *The old harridan could prove an obstacle to my plan,* Sternbye thought, *one that must be gotten around.*

Through questioning he had learned from Lord Stone that Buckley's wife had brought a small fortune with her to the marriage and that it had been improved upon. That, plus the fact that the girl proved as empty-headed as any he had ever seen, began his planning. Thus far fate had stepped to his aid, and now he plotted how to further manipulate events to his advantage, little realizing the stage was already set. Time was the only factor that he had no control over and it concerned him greatly. Already his behaviour towards the Marquess had put him in disfavour among the gentlemen; he had no doubt Lord Stone would see to his instant removal if he became suspicious of his intentions towards the girl. All his actions must be carefully considered to allay apprehension on everyone's part, he concluded. With a tug here and there, he made certain of his appearance. Assured that his orange breeches and rose-red frock coat were neat and hanging correctly, he fixed a toothy smile upon his face and set about to make himself pleasant to the older women and gentlemen, being most solicitous of the Marchioness and Lord Stone. They were almost driven to distraction by his efforts before supper was announced.

Lady Longeton accepted the arm the Marquess offered when Eaken intoned supper. "Is there still to be an announcement this eve?" he asked as she took in his brooding countenance.

He nodded curtly.

"You could delay until word reaches us. I am certain that Wenton will be able to clear the matter up for us when he arrives. He knows more of Longeton dealings than even I, especially your brother's affairs. I left the settlement of matters in his hands when Duard died, as you know. Enough then," she said, patting his arm. "Take heart—anyone who hates well also loves well," the Marchioness ended encouragingly.

Longeton and the Marchioness took their places at the long table. Changes in seating arrangements caused a flurry of activity as all sought their proper places. Lady Augusta brightened visibly as she saw that Dianna was to sit to the left of his lordship. Thomasina noted with relief and with the faint hope of reprieve that she was to sit at the far end of the table to the left of the Marchioness.

When the time came for the gentlemen to take their port, the Marquess rose. "I have a request," he said, pausing until all were listening. "This eve I desire to make an announcement, so let us all adjourn to the salon at this time.

"No, no," he answered the outburst of questions bantered at him by Lord John and Sir Peter. "You shall all know in a few moments what I wish to impart."

Waiters holding trays laden with champagne-filled glasses awaited them. Pausing until all had been served and comfortably seated, Longeton raised his glass.

"I propose a toast. Let us drink to a long and happy life for my betrothed." He walked slowly to where Thomasina sat. "To you," he said, piercing her to the quick with his emerald-green stare.

All about them was utter silence except for smothered gasps from Lady Augusta and Dianna.

"Will you not drink with me?" Longeton challenged.

Instantly, felicitations and laughter broke out. Longeton took Thomasina's hand and helped her rise. Standing at his side she was ashen, unable to speak—unable to believe he had truly done it.

After the first burst of congratulations ended, the Marquess called for silence.

"There is one present," he said, "whom I must thank, for it is she who was responsible for introducing me to Miss Thait." He bowed towards Lady Augusta. "A toast to your kindness, Baroness," he toasted, lifting his glass.

"To the Baroness," echoed about the room and all drank.

The startled lady knew not what to make of matters. All hopes crushed upon the one side and hope renewed for connections with Longeton on the other. As she tried to manage this sudden alteration with aplomb, the only matter clear to her was that Dianna would have to be severly reprimanded—both for her past treatment of Thomasina and her nitwitted dallying with Sternbye.

For Thomasina, the evening had proven a long struggle. The Marquess had not moved far from her side since the announcement and the conversation and congratulations grew increasingly unbearable.

At last Longeton was motioned away by Lord Buckley. Mathew approached, bowed, and kissed Thomasina's gloved hand. "My most sincere felicitations upon your . . .

Why, Tommi, what is the matter?" he asked as he saw the dismay in her eyes.

"Tut, tut," Sternbye clicked mockingly as he joined them. "Your claim has been overridden," he sneered derisively to Mathew.

"Why, you . . ." Mathew began, stepping towards Lord George.

"No, Mathew," Thomasina said quickly, moving between them, taking hold of Sherrad's arm.

"Of course, the 'lady' is correct, Lord Sherrad," Sternbye continued mockingly.

"Tommi, release my arm," Mathew said lowly, bristling.

"Lord Sternbye," Longeton addressed the dandy, "Lord Stone wishes to speak with you. Lord Sherrad, please excuse Thomasina; my grandmother wishes a few words," he said, taking hold of her arm.

"May I express my congratulations," Mathew said holding out his hand. "I wish you both a long and happy life together."

After hesitating momentarily, Longeton reached out and shook Sherrad's hand. The firm grip and clear, direct eye contact given by the young Viscount gave assurance of his sincerity. "Thank you," the Marquess answered, then drew Thomasina away. "Fine man, Sherrad is," Longeton commented to her as they walked across the room. "What did Sternbye say to raise his hackles so?"

Intercepted by Lord Claymore, the Marquess had to forego the answer. Thomasina nodded and attempted to smile at the appropriate times but her mind wondered at Longeton's words—what dishonourable man would commend another who was not? Glancing at him while he spoke with Lord Claymore, she noted the solid lines of his face, the lack of any sign of dissolute living. His features were not those of a man who spent his time taking the homes and means of livelihood from those weaker than he. What she felt and saw contradicted what she knew for fact—what could not be denied.

"At last, Miss Buckley, a moment to speak with you. Why have you been avoiding me?" Lord George purred.

"Why, Lord Sternbye, I would not think of choosing to be without your company," Dianna responded warmly.

"We must speak—at length," he said, lowering his voice as Lady Terese passed near them. "There is a matter of great import to you and myself which I must discuss with you."

"Whatever can you mean?" flirted the young girl as she saw Thomasina frowning at her.

"You have been so ill-used," he began. "I cannot understand how your mother—oh, pardon my words, but I cannot tolerate injustice directed at one as lovely and innocent as you," he blustered. "How can your mother force you to associate with Miss Thait? Why, even as Lord Longeton announced their betrothal, she was agreeing to an assignation with Sherrad."

"No," protested Dianna weakly.

Like a hound who has scented the fox, Sternbye pressed on. "Did you not see his reaction when I approached them?" he asked indignantly. "I only meant to offer my congratulations to Miss Thait and could not help overhearing their plans. When I mildly reproved them, well, you saw his reaction."

Her worst fears verified, Dianna shook her head. "You . . . you were brave to speak out against their designs," she said tremulously.

"It was thought of you that caused my action," Sternbye said, taking her hand in both of his. "Knowing you would never be untrue to one you loved, Miss Buckley, I could not tolerate the unfaithfulness I was witness to. May I hope that there is a chance that you shall find a place in your heart for—"

"Oh, Lord Sternbye, you must not," she interrupted him.

"Forgive me, dear Miss Buckley. I go far beyond propriety in speaking out so, I know. Just being in your presence affects me so," he sighed heavily.

Seeing her mother, Dianna jerked her hand free. Sternbye spotted Lady Augusta heading towards them. "Promise me you shall speak with me once more before you depart Thornhill. The ball Thursday eve—it would be easily accomplished with so many present. Please, favour me by this. I do not care to live if you will not," he implored.

"Of . . . of course, I shall speak with you, Lord Sternbye," she answered breathlessly, torn between his words and her mother's impending arrival. Mathew never once said anything so romantic, so thrilling, Dianna thought; the idea that Lord Longeton would even consider to express such a thought made her giggle.

"There is little for you to be laughing about," her mother piped in an undertone as she reached Dianna's side. "Not only did you lose the chance to be Marchioness, but by encouraging the attentions of that fop you have lessened your chances even with those such as Sherrad," she scolded.

"I would not have him—"

"You would not?" interrupted her mother, drawing the girl roughly aside. "How could any child of mine be such a conceited, ungrateful wretch? If you do not mend your ways, miss, not even the most generous dowry will purchase a husband for you. Why, even your behaviour towards Thomasina has been shameful."

"But mother, I only did as . . ." Dianna tried to protest.

"Silence. To your room. I shall make your apologies. Tomorrow we shall discuss your behaviour," Lady Augusta commanded in a tone that filled Dianna with foreboding.

Sulking from the salon, feeling betrayed and deserted by all, she wondered if only

Lord George saw matters in their true light. Holding to the comfort of his words, she dwelled upon thoughts of him long after she reached her room.

CHAPTER 18

Longeton's announcement caused Thomasina's circumstances to be quite altered. Awakening to a serving girl awaiting to give her hot cocoa and an abigail assigned to attend her, she recalled incidents her mother had spoken of about her life at Buckley House. In the past Thomasina had been a spectator, or provider of such services, so she allowed herself a passive enjoyment of this change in her role.

Defiance flared briefly when she found her things had been removed to a far grander room—actually a suite of rooms—for she did not feel it honest to accept such gratuities when she had no intention of marrying the Marquess. However, freedom from Dianna's self-pitying, silent, accusing presence won over her objections.

It greatly relieved Thomasina that Longeton did not press her, allowing her to come and go as she pleased during the various activities, ever the gentleman. They exchanged words during meals or when the group of young people walked or rode, but never did he go beyond generalities, in all things being ever solicitous of her in words and actions. All this only served to heighten her turmoil, increase her indecision. Adding to it further was the growing concern for Dianna.

Her cousin refused to speak more than social amenities. She would not listen to anything concerning Mathew or Sternbye. Realizing the girl had been bombarded with a new series of tirades from her mother, Thomasina ached to comfort and reassure her, to tell her that Mathew did care, but Dianna cut her off coldly whenever she broached the subject. Mathew, too, found himself instantly and cruelly snubbed in his attempts to speak with her. The growing tension showed itself in the heightened pitch of her voice, her false gaiety, and abrupt actions.

Sensing Dianna was nearing the point where she would lose control—do or say something foolish, or worse—Thomasina hovered in the background, constantly watching, concern for her cousin overriding her own anxieties for the time being.

"Mathew, have you seen Dianna?" Thomasina asked the Viscount, encountering him as she wove a path through the many people assembled for the ball Thursday evening.

"I thought I saw Sir Peter leading her out to the terrace. It is frightfully warm in here with this crush of people. Shall I help you find her?" he asked, wiping the sweat from his forehead as he spoke.

"That is not necessary. But do your best to watch Lord Sternbye. He makes me very uneasy. I feel as if something is going to occur this night."

"You should have let me 'manage' him two nights past," Mathew answered darkly. "But you worry overly much. He has kept from

Dianna and I am certain Lady Augusta will keep her on a short rein."

"Why, are you not concerned?" Thomasina questioned. "Have your feelings for Dianna altered?"

"Of course not, but nothing is to be gained from any action on my part. You have seen how she smiles at that Sternbye fellow and cuts me. After we return home and she has had time to think—then I shall speak with her."

Frowning at the wisdom of his words, Thomasina was about to answer Mathew when Lord John came and demanded she join the minuet with him.

While she danced with him, then Sir Peter, and other friends of the Marquess, she caught glimpses of Lord George and Dianna—always with others for partners, but her uneasiness would not be set aside.

"I have been ordered to fetch you," Sir Peter bowed before Thomasina as Lord Claymore lead her from the dance.

With a smile at the older gentleman, she excused herself and gladly took Sir Peter's arm. "How kind of you to rescue me, sir," she said with relief. "In truth my feet can take little more."

"Have you enjoyed the evening?"

"The evening? Yes. The entire week has been a delight."

"Thank you, Peter," a voice intruded. "Thomasina, I thought you might have need of this," the tall figure added, holding a glass of champagne out to her.

Caught off guard, Thomasina flashed a warm smile of gratitude. Their eyes caught and held each other.

"Ah, well, yes," Sir Peter stumbled verbally as he watched the pair. "I shall excuse myself then, unless I can be of service?"

They heard him not. Chuckling, he walked away.

"Would you like to take a turn on the terrace?" the Marquess spoke at last. "The evening is very warm and I would not want you to become overheated. Grandmother has been thrilled at the turnout—a 'true crush' as she would say."

Allowing him to lead the way, Thomasina's heart bade her to forget the past—to judge her love on what she saw and felt now, in the present. Perhaps it was a similar name to the

Marquess's that had been said and her mother had misunderstood it, she thought, grasping for any justification to follow her heart.

The odor of liquor crossed her senses. A large man stumbled nearby and lunged at Thomasina's arm to keep from falling. Longeton in turn released her hand and grabbed the fellow.

"Why, ish Longeton," the man slurred, jerking away. "You mush give me 'tunity ta rega'n muh loses," he demanded drunkenly. "Ish only fair."

A jerk of the Marquess's hand brought two footmen. Without a word he handed the man over to them. "See he does not return," he commanded them crisply and turned back to Thomasina.

The look of abhorrence on her face struck him as no physical blow had ever done. Taking her hand, he felt it cold and unresponsive to his touch as he led her to the edge of the terrace.

"That man," she choked out, "who was he?"

"I know him not; my grandmother supervised the invitations. He probably took me for my brother. Why do you suddenly act as if

I have done some heinous deed? The footmen will only prevent him from being a nuisance to the other guests."

"And when," Thomasina said through a growing haze as she forced herself to look at him, "will you give him a chance to recover his losses? He must surely have something left you can strip him of."

"Tommi, what are you speaking of?" Longeton entreated, baffled by her words and their vehemence.

"A marriage between us can never be," she flung at him. "Have you not caused me enough grief? Why do you persist in this travesty?" Tears spilled in great droplets from her eyes.

"I do not understand," Longeton said, his voice heavy with anguish. "Tommi, please," he began, reaching for her.

"Do not touch me," Thomasina said, barely above a whisper. "Leave me—now—I beg you."

Longeton could not bear the look on Thomasina's face, knowing he was powerless to comfort her. With an oath on his lips, he strode away.

Several people called to him in vain as he

made his way across the crowded ballroom. Only solid flesh and bone, as it jarred against his, halted him.

"Lord Longeton, I am sorry," Viscount Sherrad apologized. "Had my eye on Sternbye and did not see you."

"Why would you watch Sternbye?" the Marquess demanded. He cocked his head suspiciously. "Does it concern Thomasina?"

"I suppose one could say it does," Mathew answered nervously, wondering what to tell Longeton of the whole affair.

Sensing the reluctance, Longeton stared at Sherrad—reaching for a decision. "Thomasina is on the western edge of the terrace. Something has upset her. Will you see to her for me?" he asked at last. "Tell her she may retire to her room if she wishes—I will make her excuses if she does not return."

"As you wish, Lord Longeton," Mathew answered in puzzlement.

Grim-faced, Longeton acknowledged his response and excused himself.

It took Mathew some time to find Thomasina. She had left the terrace for the solitude of a bench in the garden beyond. Sitting down beside her, he said nothing, simply reaching out to take hold of her hand. After several moments, Thomasina returned his grip.

"Longeton said he would make apologies for you if you did not wish to return to the ball."

Without a glance at him, she nodded.

"You care to speak about it?"

"Maybe . . . later." Thomasina rose, a haunted look reflected in her face by the moonlight.

"Tommi . . ." Mathew began.

Shaking her head, Thomasina stepped away.

Quickly he stepped in front of her. "I do not know what is wrong between the two of you that Longeton should need to send me to comfort you, but I have no doubt that you love him, and you should realize how much Longeton must love you. Let nothing stand in your way, Tommi." He lifted her chin forcing her to look at him. "Are not Dianna and I a sad enough example?" He paused. "You will think on it?"

Thomasina nodded.

On impulse, Mathew kissed her on the cheek.

"Thank you . . . for caring about my welfare," she said with a quavering smile, reaching to return the kiss; she took his arm and they walked back towards the terrace.

"See," Lord Sternbye whispered, "it is as I said."

Dianna's last hope had been vanquished by Mathew's appearance at Thomasina's side. Until that moment she had clung to the belief that what Thomasina said was true. Now there remained no hope for her; she would be a lonely spinster as her mother had said.

"My dearest Miss Buckley," Lord George said, leading her from the shrubbery that concealed them to a spot deeper in the shadows of the garden. "Sit with me for a time. Just to gaze upon your countenance is pure delight."

The distance they were from the terrace, the total privacy of the spot, and Lord Sternbye's air of intimacy began to disturb Dianna. "Only for a moment, my lord. You know my mother will be most displeased by my absence."

"Oh, 'tis not fair you should be so persecuted," he told her passionately.

Startled, Dianna drew away from him.

"I have alarmed you, forgive me," he said in more soothing tones. "Do not you have the same yearning to be free of domination just as I do? I know what it is, for my father is much the same as your mother."

"My lord—"

"Have I said too much? Will you discard my affection?" he asked, turning from her despondently.

"My lord, I did not know . . . that you . . . suffered a like fate. I could never think less of you for that."

Swinging about, he clasped her hand and kissed it several times. "Miss Buckley," he said, staring deeply into her widening eyes, "do I dare to suggest a plan that would free us both?"

Mesmerized, Dianna said nothing as he led her to a bench and they sat.

"If you could but agree to my plan, never again would your mother be able to reprimand you." Sternbye paused to let her consider that thought. *And I would be satisfying at least part of my father's demands,* he continued to himself. "More importantly," he went on hurriedly, "I would be united to the one I love."

"United? Love?" Dianna breathed.

"Yes, my sweet. The way has been prepared. Say you will be my wife?"

"Mother would never agree . . ."

"Come with me and you would never have to think about your mother agreeing or disagreeing ever again! Race with me to Gretna Green! Once we are married, what objection could she make?" he appealed. "An estate will be mine upon my father's death and my family is very old."

All the pain, hurt, embarrassment, and humiliation of the past weeks passed through Dianna's mind. No one had consoled her—Thomasina had only lied—Lord George had been the only one consistently kind, she told herself. Certainly he must care for her. Would not he be better than never having anyone care?

"Say you will come with me," Lord George pleaded. "I have a small valise secreted near here. You can slip to your room and pack what few things you need for the journey. Bring what jewels and monies you have—we will purchase what we need as we travel.

When the guests begin taking their leave we shall meet here. I have a carriage waiting not far beyond. We will have traveled a far distance by morn. They shall not know what has happened when you are found missing; and by the time they learn what has taken place, we shall be safely wed," he exclaimed.

"What can they do but welcome us happily upon our return? Lord and Lady Sternbye—does that not have a grand ring? Come, let us show them all—say you will wed me!"

"Yes, yes, I will," Dianna responded to his eagerness.

"Keep in mind that we shall soon be on our way—free of reprimands forever," Lord George added with even more spirit to bolster her, ere she weaken in the resolve. "Let us fetch the valise. In an hour we shall be winging our way to Scotland!"

CHAPTER 19

A fitful sleep had finally overtaken Thomasina. Dreams marched to and fro as she tossed and turned until a particularly vivid one startled her to wakefulness.

"I didn't think you would ever wake, Tommi," a voice greeted her fumingly.

In the flickering candlelight, Thomasina saw a small form. Her vision adjusting, she recognized him. "Parker, what are you doing here?" she asked, shaking her head to clear it of sleep's fine web.

"You must come with me, Tommi. Something has happened to Dianna. She is gone!"

"Gone? What do you mean?"

"I was awakened by the sounds of the carriages as the last guests departed. Dianna had promised to bring some champagne to her room for me to sip, so I slipped into it to await her. I waited ever so long—I even fell asleep waiting. When I woke up she was still not there and no one was stirring—the house is dark."

"Parker, I have had enough of your pranks," Thomasina scolded the boy. "Return to your room before you arouse others."

"It is the truth, Tommi. Please—come look," Parker implored, tugging at her hand.

"Oh, all right, if only to prevent you from disturbing others. But I myself will turn you over my knee if this is another one of your antics," she warned him as she rose and pulled her dressing gown over her long nightdress. "Go quietly, now—we do not want to awaken anyone."

Their steps creaked loudly to their ears and the meager light of the single candle seemed a torch in Thomasina's hand that all should see. She shut the door of Dianna's room behind them with relief, only to have it replaced with dread as the candlelight revealed an untouched bed and open wardrobe doors, with various articles of clothing strewn about.

Thomasina's mind worked frantically; this could mean only one thing. "Parker, you return to your room and tell no one what you have seen or that you spoke to me. They probably will not think to ask you anything, so do not offer what you know."

"Where is she, Tommi? What are you going to do?" the boy asked, disliking the idea that he was to be excluded. "Has she run away at last?"

"I do not know," Thomasina answered, not daring to tell Parker what she believed. "Do as I say or you shall be in further trouble with your mother. I shall tell you all I learn at the first opportunity."

"Will you give your word that you will?"

"My word of honour. Now go off to bed—quietly." She lit a candle at Dianna's bedside. "Take your candle and be careful," Thomasina admonished, seeing him to the door. Closing it behind her, her mind raced over the possibilities open to her.

Mathew could be awakened, but that

would do little good; he had traveled with his parents and had no carriage of his own they could use. Only Longeton could arrange for a coach and four with no questions asked and with a minimum of people knowing of it.

Did she dare to ask him?

Yes, she decided. He desired marriage and till now she had refused. In return for his help in finding Dianna she would agree to it; at least then the action would not be in vain.

He could laugh in your face, her subconscious warned her.

Acknowledging that fact, she still felt it necessary to make the attempt. *I am partly responsible that she has done this*, Thomasina reasoned with herself. *If I had not agreed to Mathew's scheme nor left the ball early this eve, she would not have bolted with Sternbye.*

The thought of that pompous coxcomb decided her—action was necessary *now*. She had to save Dianna from life with that false fop.

Calm. Remain calm, she told herself. *First I must find the Marquess.*

The thought was daunting, for she had never been in a man's bedroom other than the Baron's, but by picturing her aunt's reaction in the morn, she was able to bolster her courage and stepped out into the hall.

Drawing a mental picture of the wing his rooms were in, she was thankful for the over-talkative girl who had carried her baggage to the new rooms she was given only two days before. The maid had insisted upon describing every detail of the hall and rooms where his lordship slept, and Thomasina had endured her talkativeness with a heavy heart. Now she was thankful she had put aside the urge to tell the girl to be silent.

Soon the Marquess's door was before her. Putting a hand on the knob, Thomasina raised the other to still her heart's deafening thumps. *Why did I not have Parker come with me to awaken him?* she thought. *Could I knock?*

No, that would awaken Gideon, she argued with herself.

Like a man leaping from a burning building, she opened the door and stepped in before her nerve deserted her completely.

The clank as it closed caused her to start and she found she had to stifle a nervous laugh. Why should she fear the sound would awaken him? If only it had, she thought as she edged towards the huge, canopied bed.

Only a sheet covered the long slim form of the Marquess as he lay sleeping on his stomach, his head turned from her.

Setting the candleholder on the table beside the bed, she waited, hoping the light would awaken him. A warm flush rose to her cheeks as she stared at the broad muscular back that lay bare before her. Never had she seen a man with less than a shirt, and never before had she desired to lay her hand on one's bare skin.

A strong desire to see his face as he slept came over her. Drawing nearer, she raised the candle above his head and stood on tiptoes staring down at the now relaxed, handsome face. Slowly she set the candle back onto the bedside table. "My lord," she whispered. Longeton did not stir.

With a gulp, she shook him timidly and again said, "My lord."

Longeton sprang to a sitting position and Thomasina whirled away as the sheet slipped, revealing more and more bare flesh.

"Thomasina?" Longeton asked in a strange

voice. "What has caused you to come here?" he exclaimed, his mind coming to grips with the reality of her presence.

"Dianna has run off with Lord Sternbye—or, I fear she has. She must be brought back before anyone discovers she is gone or harm is done to her," she told him, her back still turned.

Cinching the belt of his dressing robe, Longeton took hold of Thomasina's shoulders and turned her to face him.

Her face was lifted fearlessly to his, but her legs trembled so, she felt she must fall if he released her.

"You came to my room in the middle of the night to ask me to rescue your cousin?" he demanded.

Nodding, Thomasina added hastily, "If you agree to do this, I shall agree to marry you. There is no time to be lost—will you help?"

"How do you know she has gone?"

"Parker woke me. Her bed is untouched and there are signs she packed some things in a great hurry. Surely we can catch them if we are off immediately?" she asked urgently.

"You are truly this concerned for that hen-witted cousin of yours, who has been barely civil to you?" Longeton wondered aloud.

"Dianna is foolish, but who would not be with Aunt Augusta for a mother?" Thomasina rose to her defense. "Please, we must hurry!"

"I hardly think we are dressed for a mad dash after an absconding pair," he said, his smile barely traceable in the candlelight. "You are very beautiful with those tousled curls," he said, quietly reaching to touch one.

Thomasina stepped back, clasping the lapels of her dressing gown close, suddenly all too conscious of her appearance.

"Did you not once consider what would happen to your reputation if you were discovered here in such a state?

"No, you would not," he answered wryly for her. "Return to your room, dress, and meet me at the stables."

"No one must know of our errand," she admonished him.

"Care will be taken; go now," Longeton told her, handing her the candle she had brought after lighting his own.

A quick glance around his door showed the

hall still dark and empty. Thomasina sheltered the candle flame with her hand and dashed down the hall.

"Good Fortune, continue to shine on us," Thomasina said to herself as she eased out the large outer doors of Thornhill and saw the grounds bathed in moonlight. Hearing the neigh of horses and the jingle of harness, she picked up her skirts and rushed towards the stables.

"Mathew!" she exclaimed as she saw who was at the horses' heads.

"Quiet!" he warned her. "Do you wish to wake everyone?"

Longeton emerged from behind the last pair. "We are ready," he said to Sherrad. "Inside with you, Thomasina," he ordered, taking her arm and leading her to the door of the light, enclosed carriage.

With Mathew and Longeton at their heads leading them, the teams drew the light coach down the secondary path leading behind Thornhill. They halted just out of sight of the main house. Both men scrambled onto the coach box and Thomasina found herself floored by the sudden burst of speed Longeton got from the four as he urged them forward.

The journey had begun.

CHAPTER 20

The moonlight revealed the worst dangers of the road the light coach traveled, enabling Longeton to set a fast pace. Neither man spoke as they rocketed along; Thomasina was fully occupied holding onto the side straps and maintaining her seat.

As the first wavering rays of dawn lightened the horizon, Longeton drew the sweat-lathered teams to a halt before a village hostelry. Sticking out her head, Thomasina saw Mathew in earnest conversation with a man who looked to be in charge of the stables; she caught a glimpse of the Marquess as he disappeared inside the establishment. By the time he reappeared the horses had been changed and Mathew sat, reins in hand, impatient to be off.

"We should catch up with them before noon," Longeton threw at Thomasina as he mounted the box. She grabbed the strap just in time as Mathew applied the whip to the teams.

Midmorn they halted once again for a change of horses and for further information. A boy scurried from the inn shortly after Longeton entered it, bearing a cup of cool milk and hunks of cheese and bread for Thomasina. The milk was gulped down and the cup returned just as the Marquess came out. Tossing a bundle to Mathew, he vaulted onto the box. All dashed out of the way as he urged the fullest speed from the fresh steeds.

Bounced and jounced about the coach as they swerved round other coaches and carts, Thomasina began to wonder if she should have ever ventured on this journey. Longeton had said nothing about how close they were and she had long since lost all sense of direction and time.

A shout from Mathew caught her ear, and she felt a sudden surge of speed. Could they be near?

Her answer came in the form of frantic shouts, curses, and from her own eyes as Longeton maneuvered his teams ahead of a coach he was certain carried Dianna and Sternbye. His teams gaining the lead, the Marquess gradually forced the other coach to the skirt of the road. The angered driver cursed and whipped his team for more speed unavailingly.

The Marquess reined his teams expertly and was rewarded by the creak of leather and the groan of splintering wood as the coach he pressed slipped down the shoulder of the road, a wheel splitting under the strain.

Mathew jumped from the box before Longeton had managed the teams to a complete halt. He raced to the tilting coach, tore open the door, and dragged a startled Sternbye roughly from it by the lapels of his frock coat. Throwing the dandy to the ground without a glance, Mathew began to climb into the coach to reach Dianna, who was screaming hysterically.

A loud report echoed in his ears as he felt a burning sensation in his upper arm. Realizing he had been shot, Mathew turned to face his attacker just as Longeton's booted foot kicked the pistol from Sternbye's hand.

"Silence!" Lady Longeton commanded as she entered the breakfast room, her tone and presence demanding obedience.

The Baron, Baroness, Lord and Lady Sherrad, Lord John, Nicholas, and Sir Peter stared open-mouthed at her as she dismissed the servants and closed the doors.

"Now, Baron," the Marchioness ordered as she sat, "You may tell me what this furor is over."

Everyone burst into speech simultaneously.

Rapping the table with her cane, Lady Longeton achieved a degree of stillness; only Lady Augusta gasped and sobbed intermittently.

"The Baron and the Baron alone shall speak," the Marchioness ordered steelily.

"I do not know where to begin, my lady," the Baron's words stumbled out. "What can one make of this? Oh, dear, I do not know."

"If you will *tell* me what it is that has

caused your concern, perhaps I can make something of it."

Her icy tone calmed the Baron. "The truth is, your ladyship, that my daughter and niece, your grandson and young Sherrad have all disappeared during the night. Dianna's bed has not been slept in while all the others appear to have been roused from theirs.

"Lord John has just now come from the stables with the news that a coach and four are missing, and Lord Stone sent a message that Lord Sternbye has absconded with his coach and pair and heavens knows what else.

"What can it all mean?"

Fresh sobs broke from Lady Augusta.

"Stop that sniveling," Lady Longeton ordered her curtly. "I must think. John, Peter, do you know anything of the matter? Did Brutus say anything that would lead you to believe he was planning something?"

"No. Lord Sherrad spoke the evening past that he must keep an eye on Sternbye, but did not say why," Lord John offered.

Sir Peter shrugged unhelpfully.

"Nicholas—Lord Claymore, do you know anything about your son's plans?"

Both men sighed negatively.

All watched as Lady Longeton sat in deep thought. Her considerations concluded, she announced, "It is my belief that your daughter, Baron, has run off with that Sternbye fop. In all probability Brutus, Sherrad, and Miss Thait are pursuing them. We shall therefore maintain an outward calm—the girls will be said to be indisposed after the excitement of the evening—which will seem natural enough. Brutus and young Sherrad are on a drive—to try a new pair, perhaps.

"Say nothing, evade questions, and we shall come out of this, hopefully, with a minimum of scars. If they have not sent word or returned by tomorrow morn, we shall consider the matter further."

All nodded their acceptance of this plan.

"Baron Buckley, I suggest you take Lady Augusta to your rooms until she recovers sufficiently. Please send in Eaken," she added as Buckley helped his wife rise. "I am famished."

"How could she do this to me?" railed Lady Augusta at her silent husband. "She is truly a daughter of your blood. Such a selfish, trying child—to whom I have devoted my life! No thought for anyone save herself. Buckley through and through is the stupid chit. I shall be ruined when this becomes the lates 'on-dit' and you may be certain it will." She wagged her fingers at him. "I know how people talk. They shall spread this news eagerly. I can see their facs now—how they will enjoy my mortification!" Covering her eyes, she continued "Oh, why did this happen to me?" Stamping her foot, she lowered her hands.

"When I get my hands on her, I shall teach her the lesson of her life," the Baroness went on, ranting as she had done since they reached the room.

"Enough!"

"Did you speak? What have you to say?" she asked her husband with searing sarcasm.

The Baron's plump face showed the tension and fear under which he laboured. "Close your mouth, woman," he said calmly.

Lady Augusta gasped. Her mouth worked but no words came. The Baron advanced and pushed her into a chair.

"Now you will listen to me, Augusta," he

began with restrained fury. "I have heard enough of your words to last me a hundred lifetimes. If I had stopped you years ago as I had ought, our daughter would not now be in the hands of a . . . a who knows what he is—cad or worse. Have you not one thought for her? For what she may be going through?

"Wash your face. We are going to do exactly as the Marchioness has said and if—and I say 'if'—we are fortunate enough to get Dianna back, you are not going to say one harsh word to that child—not one word that is not kind nor loving. Do you understand?"

Lady Augusta stared at her husband of twenty years—suddenly a perfect stranger. Never before had he raised his voice or hand to her, nor reprimanded her in any way.

"You will do as I say," he commanded, feeling much steadier as his wife made no move to speak or act.

"Yes, my lord," she answered slowly. "Do you think she shall be returned unharmed?" she asked as she stood.

The Baron took her hand and she stepped closer to him. "I pray it be so," he said, clasping his arms about her, "I pray."

Returning his embrace, Lady Augusta laid her head upon his shoulder, something she had never done.

"Godspeed to Thomasina," she whispered.

CHAPTER 21

"That should do nicely," Thomasina told Mathew with a smile as she tied the last knot in the bandage about his arm. "Thank God his aim was as good as his choice in clothing. Here—let me help you," she admonished as he fumbled with his sleeve. Rolling it down, she fastened the links in the cuff. Immediately, Mathew sprang up and strode to Longeton's coach.

The Marquess stepped out as he neared.

"No harm done to me," Sherrad assured

him as he saw the other glance at his arm. "Dianna?"

"She is coming about. Perhaps you can prevent further hysterics," he nodded at the coach. "I shall take care of matters here and we shall be off."

"Lord Longeton . . ." Mathew began.

"I would think that after this day's work 'Brutus' would come more easily," the Marquess noted.

"It would be an honour, my lord . . . Brutus. I wish to thank you."

"Do not. It was not done on your account," Longeton replied and strode away.

"Do not soil your hands on the likes of him," he snorted at Thomasina when he saw her bent over Sternbye's prone form.

"I only wish to assure myself you have not killed him," she said, taking a last look at the split lip, the swollen cheek and eyes.

"He received better than he deserved," the Marquess scoffed.

"For once we agree," Thomasina sighed, rising. "What is to be done now?"

"We shall make all haste to return to Thornhill. It should be reached by darkness. If I have not underestimated my grandmother, she has managed it well, and we will not have been missed."

"I can never thank you—"

"You have said how you will do that," he cut her off, not unkindly.

Thomasina's eyes darkened; sadness flitted across her features, followed by despair.

"The coachman will care for Sternbye," Longeton said roughly, jarred by her look. "Let us go."

Hesitating as they reached the coach, Thomasina looked at the pair within. "May I ride with you?" she asked Longeton meekly.

"As you wish it," he answered coldly, striding to untie the teams. "Why did you not wait for me to assist you?" he asked harshly as he returned to find Thomasina struggling to mount the box. "Am I that detestable?"

"No, my lord," Thomasina mumbled as she allowed him to help her.

Longeton waited until she was settled, then calling a warning to Mathew, sent the teams off.

The wind against her face as they sped along was a relief to Thomasina. She stole glance after glance at the iron-visaged Marquess, thinking over all that had occurred since they first met.

"Bend down and cover yourself with this," Longeton ordered her, indicating his cloak on the seat between them as he slowed the teams. "It will not do to have anyone see you."

Looking ahead, she saw the village where they had last changed horses.

"Stay down and be still. I will see that the change is made with all haste."

And so it was and the same happened at the next stop. Darkness was full-fledged when Longeton drew the teams to a halt not far from Thornhill.

"You must join Dianna—in case anyone is about. Tell Mathew to join me. Here, take hold of my hand," he said as she rose to climb down.

Thomasina gripped it as she made her way over the side of the box. His strong, vibrant pulse quickened her own, and she stared at him a long moment before she made the final leap to the ground.

Having guessed Longeton's intent, Mathew stepped from the coach as she neared the door. He handed Thomasina in, a smile of happiness wreathing his face.

"Oh, Tommi," Dianna breathed as she watched her cousin settle in the seat. "I would never have believed I could be so utterly happy."

Both girls grabbed the straps as the coach lurched forward. When it was on a fairly smooth stretch, Dianna reached over and hugged her cousin warmly. "Thank you, Tommi. I can only wish you and his lordship the joy Mathew and I share. Mathew has forgiven me all and says we are to be married no matter what our parents say. Oh, how could I ever have allowed myself to be persuaded to go with Lord Sternbye? Was Mathew not marvelous? I shall never forget how he rescued me."

Sighing inwardly, Thomasina bore her cousin's constant prattle the remainder of the distance.

The coach halted just in sight of the shadowy hulk of Thornhill. The Marquess handed the reins to Mathew and stepped down. Taking Thomasina's hand as she stepped from the coach, he lead her aside and told her, "Go straight ahead—this leads to the gardens. Go through them and to the terrace. I shall cause an uproar that will draw everyone to the front of the house. When you hear the shouting, dash to your rooms. Remain there till word is sent."

Nodding, Thomasina went to Dianna, took her hand, and lead her on. Both girls turned for a last glimpse of the two men as the coach started forward.

"Hurry," Thomasina whispered and, gathering her skirts, dashed through the brush to the gardens. They paused at the edge of the terrace to catch their breath; the din to the front sent them on their way. Each leaned against the door of her rooms—Dianna longing to shout with joy, Thomasina refusing to let the tears and sobs escape.

CHAPTER 22

"And that is all there is to tell," she sighed. "I cannot believe the change in mother and it is only one day since I left. She has not said one harsh word and, unbelievably, has agreed that Mathew and I can be married this coming winter. Even Lord and Lady Sherrad were forgiving and very kind." During the pause Dianna played with the pleats of her skirt. "I . . . I want to apologize, Tommi, for . . . for all I have said and done. Can you forgive me?"

"It is all forgotten," Thomasina assured

her, rising and giving her cousin a hug. "I am very happy for you and Mathew."

"What are your plans now, Tommi? Shall you stay here or return to Buckley House until you marry?" Dianna asked.

Thomasina turned and paced distractedly away from her. "I do not know. Whatever his lordship decides. The Marchioness has mentioned you shall stay until midweek. I shall know by then."

"Is something troubling you?" Dianna asked, becoming aware for the first time of Thomasina's haggard looks and listless manner.

"What can be wrong?" Thomasina said, forcing a laugh.

"You say the name is Thait, your lordship?" Mr. Wenton asked.

"Yes. I wish to know what dealings any member of my family may have had with any member of that family."

"Thait. The name is vaguely familiar. Wait, let me go through some of the papers I brought with me." Shuffling and thumbing, the bent old man mumbled to himself. He paused and looked up. "Is this matter of import to you, your lordship?" he asked.

"Very."

"Then may I excuse myself? There are some additional papers in my room. I shall return as soon as I locate what you seek," he said, bowing.

Longeton nodded and poured himself a brandy. Taking the seat at his desk, he sipped at it slowly, allowing his thoughts to roam to Thomasina.

Some time later a knock interrupted his reverie. Mr. Wenton shuffled in when he was called. Laying an official-looking document in front of the Marquess, he explained, "This is the deed to a small tract of land and a cottage—neither of great importance nor value—which your brother won at the card table from a Sir Roger Thait. I recalled the incident when I came across this. There was some trouble collecting the deed as Thait did himself in shortly after losing the property. The matter is somewhat muddled as your brother passed away shortly after that. I hope this proves helpful, my lord."

"Helpful, indeed, Mr. Wenton. I have but one more thing to request."

"Whatever I can do," Wenton said with a staid bow.

"Deed this property to a Miss Thomasina Thait and also stipulate she is to have a livelihood of £100 yearly for her lifetime. I would make it larger but there is no need to arouse her suspicions. When you complete the work, you are to present the papers to Miss Thait—she is a guest at Thornhill at this time.

"Explain to her that you were reviewing matters of the estate and discovered that the Marquess of Thornhill had won the property dishonestly and hence it was being restored to her. Use the words 'Marquess of Thornhill' exactly. The livelihood can be said to be in reparation for damages caused by the loss of the property. Do you fathom what I wish?"

"I believe so, my lord. But is this wise or necessary?" Wenton asked. "I believe if nothing else, your brother was honest at the tables."

With a wave of his hand, Longeton dismissed the old man's remark. "I feel it necessary. See to the matter at once."

"Of course, Lord Longeton."

"Why, Mr. Wenton, you are looking well,"

Lady Longeton greeted the solicitor as she thumped into the study.

"You are most gracious, my lady, and in exceedingly good looks yourself," he responded. "If you will excuse me, I have a task to perform," he bowed.

"I hope to see you before you take your leave," she said, acknowledging his greeting. Waiting until the door closed behind him, the Marchioness asked her grandson, "Have you your answer?"

"Thomasina believes I am responsible for her father's death. He committed suicide shortly after Duard won a cottage and a small tract of land from him," Longeton replied.

"Stupid man. Now I recall it," Lady Longeton exclaimed. "The wife died upon receiving the news of her husband's death and the loss of her home—Thomasina's parents. The poor child. I shall go to her at once and explain. . . ."

"No."

"You cannot mean that."

"If she agrees to marry me thinking as she does, I will know she truly loves me. If I remove the obstacle, I would never be certain."

"This is utter nonsense."

"No, Gram. I shall relieve her of all obligations to marry me. I must do this as I see it. I ask you not to speak of anything we have discussed this eve."

"As you will, my dearest boy, but I think it absolute foolishness for you to risk your happiness so," she told him, shaking her head sorrowfully.

CHAPTER 23

Monday gave birth to a brilliant golden orb that spread its warming rays over Thornhill, proclaiming a gloriously beautiful, if warm, day.

Thomasina sought the comfort of the cool gardens in the afternoon. Mr. Wenton's news that the cottage would be returned to her was still being absorbed, and a new turmoil had arisen with the delivery of a note from the Marquess.

"Tommi! Tommi!" Mathew called as he ran into the garden.

"Here," she called, rising.

"Is it true what I just heard?" he asked excitedly. "Let us sit. You must tell me all. Has everything been restored to you?"

"The cottage—the land, and more," Thomasina answered slowly as they sat. "I am to be given a livelihood for my lifetime. I can be independent if I will it."

"Independent? But what of your betrothal to Longeton?" he asked. Seeing her hesitation, he reached for her hand. "There is much you have not told me. Will you trust me now?"

"I must turn to someone—if only to speak of it this once before I turn away from it all." Thomasina bit her lip as she sorted out the words.

"I believe," she said, "that the Marquess has arranged for the return of the cottage and the livelihood so that he can be free of me. Of course his solicitor would not admit that the Marquess was responsible; he said he came upon the error doing routine examination of the estate records."

"It is nonsense to say Longeton wishes to be rid of you," Mathew scoffed. "The man loves you."

"Then why did he write me this?" she said, tears brimming, as she pulled a crumpled piece of paper from her reticule.

Smoothing it straight across his knee, Mathew read:

> My dear Miss Thait,
>
> It is obvious that you find my very presence repulsive. With great sadness, therefore, I release you from any and all obligations you may feel towards me in the matter of marriage. I shall place the matter in your hands. If you depart with the Buckleys on the morrow, I shall know you have decided your happiness lies elsewhere.
>
> BL

"This has upset you?" Mathew asked, studying her with a puzzled expression upon his face.

"No . . . well, yes. Oh, Mathew, you cannot understand what torture I have been going through." She lowered her eyes. "You know I love him, but you do not know that he was responsible for my parents' deaths. His solicitor's turning over of the deed is a final admittance of his guilt. All along he had denied knowing what I was speaking of and acted as if he did not recall my father. Worse, just when I decided there must have been some mistake—that he could not have been what I imagined before I knew him—he confirms all my worst fears with this."

Mathew shook his head. "Tommi, look at me. That is better. I have not followed all of what you have said clearly, so let me ask a question. You believe it was Brutus Longeton who caused your father's death?"

Sadly, she nodded.

"Why do you think that?" he asked curiously.

"Because my mother told me that it was Marquess Longeton who had won all we had."

"Ah ha! That explains it. It was the Marquess who won it—but it was Brutus's brother, Duard, who had the title then. Brutus himself was out of the country with the army. He could not tolerate his brother's way of life and returned only after his brother died."

"You are certain?" Thomasina asked, hope lighting her face.

"I overheard my parents discussing it shortly after your arrival at Buckley House. What you must have gone through believing as you did," he said shaking his head.

"But," he brightened, "it will all end well."

"That is even worse. What a muddle I have made," Thomasina said sadly. "I cannot tell him I thought him a gambler, a cheat—worse. He will not believe I was willing to accept him before I learned the truth. In fact, he must have written the note because he no longer cares for me—if he ever has."

"Do not tell him anything," Mathew told her. "Simply remain when the Buckleys depart."

"That would not do. He will know there has been a change and I cannot lie. I am certain now he is depending upon my departing with them. It is hopeless."

"Nothing is ever hopeless," Mathew replied. "There is some way to right things—you shall see."

CHAPTER 24

Sparkling crystals of dew greeted Tuesday's rising sun, but for Thomasina the sun could not shine through her personal gloom. No solution that was satisfactory had she arrived at, and it was with a deep sigh of sadness and regret that she ordered her things packed and added to the Buckleys' baggage. The deed was done by midmorn; as they were not to depart until after a cold collation at noon, Thomasina sought the refuge and solitude of the gardens.

Here she chose a bench to one side and,

sitting, once again began to go over all the arguments for remaining. Deeply preoccupied she did not see the three gazing at her from behind a large clump of birch.

"Parker, do you understand what you are to do?" Dianna asked in a whisper.

"It shall be easy," he whispered back.

Both looked to the third conspirator.

"We are agreed then?" Mathew asked Dianna.

Smiling, she nodded.

"All right. Parker, you wait until I reach the house—then begin. Dianna shall whistle when I return—you know what to do then."

The boy's eyes sparkled in anticipation as he signed that he did.

"Be certain to return to the others as soon as you signal Parker," Mathew bade Dianna. "I shall be there to help you as soon as I can."

"Parker, go on," Dianna whispered as she saw Mathew's back disappear from view.

With a wave he trotted off. "Hello," he bade Thomasina as he skipped past her.

"Parker, where are you going? Were you not to remain in your room until we depart?" Thomasina asked, rising and following him.

"I did not care for the room—not when the

day is as lovely as this. Will you play tag with me, Tommi?" he asked, running further ahead.

"Not today, Parker, it would only get us both into trouble. Perhaps after we return to Buckley House."

"Mother will only send you away when we return home—you know she has said that. Come—find me!" he shouted and scooted out of sight.

"Come back here, Parker!" Thomasina shouted, knowing he would not. She turned back towards the bench, then, with a grimace, gave chase.

The path Parker wended through the gardens lead steadily towards a lake at the far end. As a sharp, clear whistle sounded, he dashed straight for it.

Thomasina sprinted as she saw him waver at the lake's edge. A brick wall had been built to prevent the water from wearing away the soil, and he tottered on it, flailing his arms wildly. "Tommi!" he screamed as he toppled into the water.

"Did you hear something?" Mathew asked Longeton as they came into the gardens.

"No. What was it we had to come here to speak of?" the Marquess asked irritably; he had seen Thomasina's baggage added to the Buckleys' and had been fighting the urge to speak with her ever since.

"I am certain someone is calling. Listen carefully," Sherrad urged.

A faint "Parker" came to their ears.

"The boy was to remain in his room." Longeton dismissed it with a wave of his hand.

"If you believe he would do as he was told or was 'supposed to' you do not know him as I do," Mathew noted. "What is at the end of the gardens?"

"A lake."

"Very deep?"

"Do not tell me," the Marquess said exasperatedly, "Parker cannot swim."

"Oh no, Parker swims quite well," Mathew answered innocently. "But that was Thomasina's voice we heard calling and she cannot."

"She cannot?!"

Mathew nodded. A broad grin spread across his face as Longeton began a hasty sprint towards the lake.

At lakeside, Thomasina watched as Parker floundered. It was too far back to the house to summon aid, and she knew no one was in hearing distance of her calls. But it would do little good to jump in, she reasoned, since she could not swim.

Sitting on the edge of the wall, her legs dangling in the water, she stretched as far as she could, trying to reach the boy, but he bobbed further and further away.

Desperate, she slipped from the wall and found the water to be only knee-deep; walking until it neared her waist, she called to him to try and reach her. The weight of her skirts tugged at her, causing her to lurch forward.

"Tommi!"

Longeton's desperate call turned her head and she felt a vast wave of relief and happiness flow through her as she saw his running figure.

"Parker," she called stepping back, but the boy was no where to be seen. "Parker!" she screamed, scanning the water's surface.

No answer came. Parker did not reappear, but a weight hit Thomasina in the knees from behind and down into the water she went.

Coughing and spluttering, she pushed her head above the water. The first thing she saw was Parker's beaming face, the next, a split second later, was Longeton taking a flying dive into the lake in her direction. The force of his body hitting the water combined with the weight of her wet skirts threw Thomasina back and under the water again.

Her head above the surface once more, Thomasina did not know if she should laugh or cry as she saw the terrified look on the Marquess's face as he hunted for sight of her across the water's surface. Seeing her, his face was illuminated with joy. In a few strokes he reached her side and swept her into his arms, crushing her in a thankful embrace. As he hugged her, he discovered the water was just below his chest and he could stand easily. Swinging his gaze at Parker, the boy grinned in return.

Steadying Thomasina as she gained her feet and tried to step forward, their eyes met and held.

"Thank God you are safe," he breathed as if it were a miracle.

"You do care," Thomasina cried joyfully, reaching to touch his cheek.

"Care?! Do you know how I love you?" he asked, drawing her to him once more, easing his hold only so he could kiss her.

Neither heard the three hoots Parker sounded in the direction of the house.

Mathew, standing before the opened outer doors of the main salon, heard the hoots. He walked over and addressed Eaken. "Please see that Miss Thait's baggage is returned to her rooms," he instructed.

"But she said she was returning with us," Lady Augusta objected.

"There has been a slight change in her plans, mother," Dianna explained. "Thomasina indicated that she would remain here until the decision was made as to when their wedding would be."

"When was this? I am certain . . ." Lady Augusta began.

"Augusta," the Baron said warningly.

The Baroness looked to her husband. "It must be as you say, Dianna."

Eaken shrugged inwardly at this supposedly meaningful exchange. One never knows what the gentry are about, he thought as he went to do as Mathew had bid.

"You should fetch Thomasina in from the garden, Dianna. The time we have left is growing short and I would like to visit with her before we go," Lady Augusta told her daughter.

"Oh, I do not think she is in the garden any longer," Dianna answered. "She will join us in good time for a visit."

"Yes, you know she would not fail to bid Parker farewell," Mathew added, taking a seat beside Dianna and winking at the Marchioness, who had been observing the exchange of looks between the two.

The Baroness also wondered at the strange exchange of glances between them, but passed it off as lovers' understandings. Thinking her son safely in his room, she sighed. At least he was out of mischief for once, she thought.

A faint smile hid the Marchioness's thoughts. Wondering just what the young couple had put Parker up to, she thanked God that the problem had evidently been resolved. Another point for me, she noted mentally. I wonder if Jane favours a girl or boy for her wager as choice for their first?

Thomasina drew back, breathless. "I must tell you," she began but was silenced by a brief kiss. "Now, Lord Longeton, you must listen."

In answer he kissed her again.

"You must know what I thought of you," she tried again.

"I care only if you love me and *I* think you are the most beautiful woman in the world. Besides"—he kissed the tip of her nose—"I know what you think. And now that I am certain of your love I can tell you that it was not I, but my brother, who gambled with your father. And the man who demanded a chance for regaining his losses? He was another of Duard's victims. He was so drunk he mistook me for him."

Gazing into those deep emerald eyes, Thomasina decided there was no need to tell him that she had known all. It was enough that he was satisfied.

"Let us put all misunderstandings behind us," he told her, "forever."

"Oh, yes," she answered.

"Is that all you two are going to do?" Parker asked indignantly from where he sat upon the wall's edge. "How am I to have any fun?"

As one, Thomasina and Longeton turned towards the boy, scooping and splashing water at him. The wet skirts wrapped around Thomasina's legs as she stepped forward, causing her to fall. Longeton caught her and lifted her in his arms, slogging through the water to the wall.

Must they always stare at each other so? Parker asked himself in disgust. "No fun at all anymore," he tossed at them as he rose and sloshed towards the house.

"Do you recall the first time you 'fell' into my arms?" Longeton asked Thomasina as he climbed out of the water and joined her.

"Yes," she smiled, "and the second time, and the third."

Hugging her to him once again, they stood, kissing with a growing passion as the water streamed and dripped to the ground.

As they parted reluctantly, Thomasina said with a teasing glint in her eye, "We could keep Parker with us."

"I doubt that will be necessary," Longeton quipped in return, "if my children take after their mother." His features ,slowly waxed from the joy of mutual teasing to its former broodiness.

"They will not be too much like me," Thomasina earnestly assured him.

"It would please me if they were exactly like you," he told her softly. "Will you love me always, Tommi—always?"

"Forever," Thomasina breathed and drew his head to hers until their lips met and lingered, everything forgotten in their knowledge of the present and their hope in the future.